Victorio's war
Wilson, John

880L

D1605905

# VICTORIO'S
# WAR

# VICTORIO'S WAR

## JOHN WILSON

ORCA BOOK PUBLISHERS

**Library and Archives Canada Cataloguing in Publication**

Wilson, John (John Alexander), 1951-
Victorio's war / John Wilson.
(The desert legends trilogy ; v. 3)
Other volumes in trilogy: v. 1 Written in blood ; v. 2 Ghost moon.

Also issued in electronic format.
ISBN 978-1-55469-882-0

I. Title.  II. Series: Wilson, John (John Alexander), 1951- .Desert legends trilogy ; v. 3
PS8645.I4674V53 2012          JC813'.6          C2011-907537-7

First published in the United States, 2012
**Library of Congress Control Number**: 2011942580

**Summary**: Now a scout for the Army, in 1880, Jim Doolen finds himself caught
in the middle of a brutal war with Victorio's Apaches along the Mexican border.

MIX
Paper from
responsible sources
FSC® C016245

*Orca Book Publishers is dedicated to preserving the environment and has printed
this book on paper certified by the Forest Stewardship Council®.*

Orca Book Publishers gratefully acknowledges the support for its publishing programs
provided by the following agencies: the Government of Canada through the Canada Book
Fund and the Canada Council for the Arts, and the Province of British Columbia
through the BC Arts Council and the Book Publishing Tax Credit.

Cover design by Teresa Bubela
Cover photo by Getty Images
Author photo by Katherine Gordon
Poem credit: Ball, Eve. *In the Days of Victorio: Recollections of a Warm Springs Apache.*
Tucson: University of Arizona Press, 1972.

ORCA BOOK PUBLISHERS          ORCA BOOK PUBLISHERS
PO Box 5626, Stn. B                        PO Box 468
Victoria, BC  Canada                      Custer, WA  USA
v8R 6s4                                          98240-0468

www.orcabook.com
Printed and bound in Canada.

15  14  13  12  •  4  3  2  1

*For all the storytellers who help us remember.*

# Chihuahua City, Mexico

**19 October, 1880**

I am swimming through a sea of anger. Everywhere I look are waving fists, glaring eyes and shouting mouths, lips twisted back to expose rotted teeth. Above the screams of hate, the bells in the twin towers of the church across the square ring joyously. For me they sound a funeral knell for all my dead friends.

At least I am on horseback, above the seething waves of loathing. It is much worse for the sixty-eight women and children who stumble along behind me, jostled, spat on and abused by the crowd, and with only a harsh lifetime of slavery to look forward to.

Ahead of me ride the victorious soldiers, proud in their red, blue and gold uniforms and graciously accepting the flowers thrown at them by the adoring *señoritas*. They are conquering heroes, returning from a great battle that has made the land safe for everyone. To prove it, they carry poles decorated with the scalps and sun-dried, withered heads of their enemies.

I've been in this land for three years. There have been ups and downs—this is the bottom. I have been surrounded by friends and I have been lonely. Now my friends are gone and I'm alone. I've tried to do the right thing and I've made mistakes—yet everything has fallen apart regardless of what I do. I came down here from Canada looking for my father and discovered horrors I couldn't have imagined. I tried to find honest work and watched greed allow good men to be murdered and cold-eyed killers to walk free. Finally, I found the life I thought I wanted, only to be disillusioned once more in a welter of blood and death.

What's left? I don't know and, to be honest with myself, I no longer care. I'm a prisoner but I'm white. Unlike the others, I won't be sold into slavery. Sooner or later I'll be released, at least physically. Emotionally and mentally, I'll never escape from the things I've seen and done. I'll carry them with me as long as I live.

I'm so busy wallowing in my own self-pity that I don't notice the one friendly face in the crowd. It's a face I should recognize. It belongs to a man, a gentleman, whose story helped me discover my father and at whose house I recovered after the discovery—Luis Santiago de Borica. Fortunately, Santiago sees me and limps through the rowdy crowd to my prison.

The soldiers don't seem to know what to do with me. The women and children who are soon to be sold into slavery are easy. They are herded together into an old cattle corral where they sit in the dirt, huddled in small pathetic groups.

The soldiers seem quite happy to allow me to busy myself tending to Coronado, brushing him down and ministering to the cuts and scrapes he has picked up in the past few weeks. One man even gives me some salve and shows me where I can find food and water. He's young and smiles a lot, but I remain silent and stone-faced. He's showing far greater kindness to my horse than anyone is showing to the pitiful collection of human beings in the corral.

I have done all I can for Coronado and am standing absently stroking his neck when the boy I rescued at Tres Castillos—I never did discover his name—arrives with an important-looking officer.

"*Éste es el americano,*" the boy says.

The officer is immaculately dressed in a spotless uniform hanging with gold braid. He tilts his head back slightly and stares arrogantly at me down his long, aristocratic nose. "You saved this boy's life?" he asks.

"Yes."

The officer nods almost imperceptibly. "Why were you riding with the Apaches?"

"It's a long story." I don't want to get into a complicated conversation with this haughty man, and I remember Nah-kee-tats-an's advice not to be too eager to share your stories with strangers.

"*Es buen hombre,*" the boy says. *He's a good man.*

The officer looks at me as if he doubts very much whether anyone as filthy and ragged as me can possibly be a good man. "I am Colonel Joaquin Terrazas," he says. "I saw once what Apaches can do and I swore vengeance. I did not rest until I came to Tres Castillos and finally had my revenge. I do not look kindly upon those who ride with the Apaches, even Americanos."

"He's a good man," the boy repeats. "*No es Apache. Me salvó la vida.*"

Colonel Terrazas looks at the boy and then back at me. He already knows I'm not an Apache, but the fact that I saved the boy's life seems to carry some weight. "Very well then. On this boy's word, and because his uncle is an important man in this town, you may take your horse and go. I strongly suggest that you head north and do not concern yourself any further in the affairs of Mexico." He turns on his heel and stalks off.

"*Gracias, amigo,*" I say to the boy. "*¿Estarás bien?*" I ask if he will be all right.

A look of sadness flashes across the boy's face, but he hurriedly replaces it with a smile. "*Sí. Mi tío y mi tía van a cuidarme.*"

I'm glad that he has relatives to look after him. "*Bueno.*" We stand as an awkward silence grows between us. What else is there to say? We're both going back to our own different worlds.

"*Adiós,*" the boy says eventually. "*Gracias por su ayuda.*"

"*De nada,*" I say as the boy turns away. "*Momentito.*" The boy turns back. "*¿Cuál es tu nombre?*"

"Miguel," the boy replies. "*¿Y el suyo?*"

"James Doolen," I reply. "Jim."

The boy nods. He looks much older than his years. Then he's gone. I'm alone again.

I'm busy saddling Coronado when I hear Santiago's voice. "It does not look as if time has been kind to you, James Doolen."

Raw emotion floods over me. This white-haired man standing before me, leaning on a silver-headed cane, is the one true friend I have left in the world. I feel like embracing him, but I don't. Despite his threadbare clothes and scuffed boots, he has a formal, aristocratic air that will not allow such a blatant display of sentiment. Instead I shake his hand, smile and say, "You are wrong, Santiago, time *has* been kind to me. It has led me, once more, to you."

Santiago nods acknowledgment. "In that case, you must allow me to take you from this place and buy you a decent meal."

A decent meal with an old friend sounds wonderful, but I feel guilty. I glance over at the women and children in the corral. They sit around in small groups, staring dejectedly at nothing as they await their fate. The girl whose mother I saw killed stands apart from the others, staring over at Santiago and me through the wooden railings.

"My friend," Santiago continues, "would it help you or them if you were in there as well? If I have learned one thing in my time on this earth it is that life is not fair. All we can do is the best we can within the limits of the possible. There is nothing you can do for them."

I know he's right, but I have shared much with these people and it is difficult to leave them to their fate. I raise my hand and wave at the girl. She doesn't move, standing like a statue and staring impassively back. Santiago gently takes my arm. "Bring Coronado," he says. "We will put him in the livery stable, and then we shall eat at the hotel where I stay. The food is not what Maria could cook, but it is palatable."

"Maria is here as well?" I ask.

"Maria went to God this past winter," Santiago explains. "It was for the best. Every day her mind spent less and less time in this world. She was back at the Governor's Palace in Monterey. At the end she did not even recognize me because I do not resemble the young man from those times."

"I am sorry to hear that," I say as we begin to move slowly out of the compound.

"Do not be," Santiago says. "The next world comes to us all sooner or later."

"Why are you in Chihuahua?" I ask.

"I came to see the *medico* here. I have had many pains over the years, in my leg all my life and in my joints more recently. I am used to them, but a new pain appeared last year in my chest. The *medico* confirmed what I suspected, that my old heart has had enough and is in need of a rest. I came to see the *medico*, but I stay to settle my affairs."

Santiago raises a hand to prevent my expression of regret. "Do not drown me in sympathy. I have had a long life filled with good and bad, pleasure and pain. I am ready to take my ease in whatever the next world offers. Besides, I am lonely. I no longer have Maria to share things with. The *medico* says there is a good chance that I will not suffer, that my poor old heart will simply just stop. That does not seem such a bad way to exit this life, so I will wait and accept what comes.

"But in the meantime," Santiago says brightly, "let us at least enjoy a good meal and share some stories."

—✦—

I sit back replete and pat my belly, the first time it has been full in weeks. I push away the guilt I feel at being well fed while so many are starving and thank Santiago.

"You are welcome, James," he says, "but little is free in this world. You must pay me back for this."

"I will get some work and earn enough to return your kindness," I promise.

Santiago laughs. "I am not talking about money. I have a few dollars saved, not a lot, but enough that I do not need to worry about the cost of a meal or two for an old friend. What I require from you in payment is a story, perhaps more than one.

"When you showed up on my doorstep in Esqueda three years ago, a naive youth with no knowledge of the heights or depths that men can achieve, I fed you a meal and you told me of the story you were pursuing. We discovered that our stories were connected and that my story was a help to you in your quest. That forged a link between us.

"Once you discovered the answers you sought, you returned and once more I fed you. In exchange you told me how the story of your father ended. Now three years have passed, and again we sit across a table filled with empty dishes. You owe me a story."

"I do," I agree, returning Santiago's smile. "But three years is a long time, and I have many stories."

"Then I shall buy you a meal for each one. I have the time to listen. My room here is large and there is a chaise longue that I suspect will prove to be more comfortable than anything you have slept on in the past few weeks. Do we have an agreement?"

"We do," I say. "Thank you." It won't be easy telling some of the stories that have been my life for the past three years, but I cannot refuse this kind old man. "After I left Esqueda three years ago, I rode up to Lincoln in search of work. On the way, I met Bill Bonney..."

## 20 October, 1880

All day I tell Santiago the tale of my time in Lincoln, of John Tunstall's murder, of the war that resulted from that and of the final battle in Alex McSween's house in Lincoln. I tell him about Bill. How one minute he could be a charming friend, always ready for a song or a dance, and the next a cold-blooded killer. I tell of my attempts to get away from the war, but how it always surfaced when I least expected it and dragged me back in. Santiago listens to me with patient interest, only occasionally interrupting the flow to ask for clarification of some point I have not explained clearly.

As the story progresses, I begin to ramble, to branch off into unimportant side alleys. Santiago notices. That evening, after I have spent the best part of an hour philosophizing about the nature of good and evil and how Bill could be both at the same time, Santiago interrupts me. "You do not wish to tell me the next piece of the story."

He's right. After I escaped from Lincoln and became a scout for Lieutenant Fowler and the 10th Cavalry, I started on the path that led me here and left almost everyone I cared about dead. I have no wish to revisit that.

"Stories are life," Santiago says. "If we do not give them the freedom of telling, they sit and fester within us until the poison warps us and distorts what we are and what we have been."

Santiago is not the first person to tell me this. Wellington, Too-ah-yay-say, when I first met him, told me much the same. He said we were defined by our stories and that each of us were no more than the stories that made us. Our stories are important. Why else had I left a comfortable life in Yale in Canada to come down to this harsh land? I came to discover my father's story and, in doing so, my own.

Stories must be shared and exchanged with our friends. Wellington had kept Perdido's story alive and passed it on to me. Now, even though Perdido has been dead for centuries and his body ashes, he is still alive because I know his story. However hard the telling might be, my story needs to be told, not only so that I can be released from it, but also because it will ensure that my friends who passed through it will live on.

"Very well," I agree, "but I warn you, it will cost many meals, and I cannot begin tonight. I am tired and there is something I must do before I begin."

Santiago nods agreement, and I stand up and walk out into the cool evening air. I walk through the streets, ignoring the life going on around me, until I arrive at the corral where the captives are being held. They are to be sold at auction in two days' time.

I lean on the fence and let my gaze wander over the sad mass of humanity. The prisoners have been given blankets, food, and pots and pans. Small groups sit around small fires. It does not pay to mistreat them—healthy slaves are worth more.

A small figure detaches itself from a nearby group and comes over to stand hesitantly before me. It's the girl I waved to earlier. This time she grins at me, her teeth gleaming white in the dusk. I smile back.

The girl speaks no English, but I have picked up quite a bit of Apache in the past few weeks, not enough to say what I want to, but in a mixture of broken Apache, Spanish and English, and with many hand movements and gestures, I talk to her anyway.

"I have met an old friend," I say. The girl listens intently. "I have agreed to tell him my story, because stories are important. Part of what I will tell him tomorrow will be the stories of people who are dead, so that they will be remembered, but part of it will be your story, part of the story of your people.

"I am not of your people, I come from far to the north, but stories do not respect the boundaries between nations. The story I will tell will be true to me, and I shall do my best to make it true for you as far as I can. That is the best I can promise. Will that be all right with you? I would like your permission to tell the part of the story that is yours." It's stupid, asking this of the orphan girl who can understand little of what I am saying, but it's something I have to do.

For a long moment we stand looking at each other, waiting for something to happen. Then the girl digs into the wide red belt wrapped around her waist and brings out a tiny doll. It's no more than two inches high and simply made. A piece of black deer hide is wrapped like a cloak around a stick that is carved into a round head at one end. The head has a face crudely drawn on it, and long black hair hangs down on either side. A few beads are woven into the hair, and the broken quill of a feather hangs from the back.

I've seen this doll before. As far as I understand it, it represents Raven, the spirit messenger between our world and the other and the bringer of awareness. The girl holds it out to me.

"For me?" I ask.

The girl nods.

I take the doll gently. "Thank you," I say. "I will treasure it, as I will treasure your story."

The girl smiles shyly and turns back to the nearest fire. Deep in thought, I wander over to the livery stable to say good night to Coronado.

"We'll be here for a couple of days more," I say as I stroke his neck. "I have a story to tell. In any case, the rest will do us both good." Coronado nuzzles my shoulder. "I don't know what we'll do then," I reply. "Head north, I suppose. What alternative do we have?" Coronado stamps his hoof. "We'll see what happens, but I need to go now. I need as much sleep as I can get tonight. It will be hard to tell our stories tomorrow."

I move outside. It's dark now except for lantern light seeping out of nearby windows. I notice the rich smell of chili-spiced stew cooking and hear the sounds of quiet voices discussing mundane events. Somewhere far off, someone is beginning to pick out a tune on a guitar. I walk slowly back to the hotel, the weight of the past—my past and all the other pasts I have been a part of—hanging heavy on my shoulders. I will try to tell the truth tomorrow; it's the best I can do. I hope it's enough.

## 21 October, 1880

After breakfast, Santiago and I sit side by side on the bench outside the door of the hotel. It's pleasantly cool this early and the bustle of the city is just beginning. I didn't sleep well last night, lying in the dark thinking through the tale I must tell.

"The story I am going to tell you is long and in many pieces," I say. Santiago nods. "It begins where I finished last night with the battle in Lincoln, where McSween was killed. I will not dwell on the year following that. I went to Fort Stanton and Lieutenant Fowler arranged for me to be taken on as a scout with his cavalry troop.

"At first the life was hard, a lot of riding back and forth across the countryside chasing the shadows of off-reservation Apache bands, never seeing any, other than occasional distant figures on horseback who disappear long before we reach them. There was very little fighting, occasional long-range rifle fire that did no harm, but we did come upon a burned-out ranch and had the sad task of burying the charred bodies of the family we discovered in the ruins.

"It took a lot of getting used to the army, but I was lucky. As a civilian, I had more freedom than the troopers. I could be much less formal with the officers, and Fowler, through all the help he gave me, became a close friend. I think he treasured the evenings when we would sit and talk as much as I did.

"I also learned to deeply appreciate the dedication and efficiency of Sergeant Rawlins and the Buffalo Soldiers. They accepted me readily enough. All were either ex-slaves or men who had seen the depths of life in the slums and factories of New York. They treasured life in the army that gave them freedom and a level of respect they could expect in few other places. Like me, they loved the wide-open spaces of this harsh land we found ourselves in.

"For the most part, the Buffalo Soldiers were easy going and, like Bill had been, ready to break into a song or a story at any excuse. However, when we went out on patrol, they were relentless, ignoring the inevitable hardships of traveling fast over difficult country and fighting fearlessly in the minor skirmishes when we caught up with bands of escapees from the reservations.

"That year taught me a lot. It toughened me, both physically and mentally, and I came to know the countryside of Lincoln County as well as anyone not an Apache.

"Over that year, stories also reached me of Bill and his adventures. He still rode with the survivors of the Regulators, stealing cattle and horses and hunting down anyone he thought had something to do with John Tunstall's murder. In the spring of 1879, he was back in Lincoln, testifying against Dolan in an enquiry set up by the new governor, Lew Wallace. He received an amnesty for that, but as soon as Wallace left to return to Santa Fe, the charges against Dolan were dropped and the amnesty for Bill revoked, so he took to the hills again.

"Oddly, over that year I missed Bill. I knew he could be a cold-hearted killer and he got me into a lot of trouble that I was lucky to escape from alive, but he's also the most charming person I've ever met. The last thing I want to do is ride with his gang again, but I will be sad when he is eventually cornered and killed, as seems inevitable unless he flees to Mexico or somewhere else far off.

"Nothing major occurred during that year of scouting, and the troop only suffered a few men wounded. In the summer of 1979, something changed. The government offered Victorio and his band of Warm Springs Apaches a place on the Mescalero reservation around Blazer's Mill. It was a compromise between trying to force them onto the hated desert reservation at San Carlos in Arizona Territory and having them on the loose in the mountains of the Black Range at Warm Springs.

"Victorio accepted the deal and moved his people to the valleys and hills around Blazer's Mill with promises to keep the peace. It seemed as if the worst of the troubles were over. In reality they were just beginning."

Now I'm launching into the meat of my story, and as I talk, the Chihuahua street in front of me fades and I drift back to Fort Stanton as August turned to September, 1879, the start of the hardest year of my life.

# Fort Stanton, New Mexico Territory

2 September, 1879

"**I**f you set off right away and travel light, you should make Blazer's Mill before nightfall tomorrow."

I'm standing by the livery stable at Fort Stanton, and Lieutenant Fowler's giving me orders.

"I'll bring the troop down as fast as I can," he says, "but we won't be there before the day after tomorrow at the earliest, and I need to know what's going on down on the reservation as soon as possible."

"I thought Victorio and his band were settling in well down there. Is there trouble?"

"I'm not sure," Fowler explains. "Victorio seemed to be settling in, but a group of ranchers has filed a writ for his arrest on some old, vague murder charge. I'm afraid that, as soon as he hears about it, he'll lead his people back to the Black Range, and then we'll have to begin hunting him all over again."

"But it makes no sense. The ranchers and their cattle are safe as long as Victorio's happy on the reservation. If they force him off, there'll be raiding and deaths again."

"I know," Fowler says, staring off at the low morning sun in the east. "I'm afraid there's more to it than that."

"I don't understand."

Fowler turns his head and meets my eyes. He looks sad. "If Victorio settles down on the reservation, then there won't be such a need for the army. We'll go back to Texas, and there will only be a small force to keep an eye on things."

I nod, but I'm still frowning in puzzlement.

"The army goes through a lot of supplies," Fowler continues, "feed for the horses and men. And we employ a lot of men—woodcutters, blacksmiths, butchers, scouts, like you." He smiles at me. "If the army leaves, all that money and work go with us."

At first what Fowler is saying doesn't make sense, but then understanding dawns. "Are you suggesting that someone is trying to stir up trouble and force Victorio to leave the reservation just so the army will stay around and buy more supplies?"

"That's exactly what I'm saying."

"Who?"

"Who has a monopoly on supplying the army since Tunstall and McSween were killed?"

"Dolan?"

Fowler nods. "And the other business interests from Santa Fe who support him."

"But that's insane. If Victorio goes back to raiding, people will die—soldiers, ranchers, travelers, innocent women and children. For what, a few sacks of horse feed?"

"It's more than a few sacks of feed. There's big money in army contracts, especially if the officer in charge is sympathetic, but you're basically right."

"I don't believe it."

Fowler smiles. "You're a smart kid, Jim Doolen, and you've turned into a good scout in the past year, but I would have thought your time with the Regulators would have taught you more of what men are capable of when a profit's at stake. It's more than just supplying Fort Stanton. The Santa Fe ring controls the army supply for all of Arizona and New Mexico Territories and most of west Texas. That's enough money to keep a lot of people in fine houses and line the pockets of a lot of judges, politicians and lawmen. Those dime novels you read paint this land as a wide-open frontier where a man can be free. The only people free hereabouts are the likes of your friend Bill Bonney, and his days are numbered. Sooner or later he'll be hunted down, just like Victorio will be if he leaves the reservation. Only difference is, the reservation waiting for Bonney when they catch him is a deep hole in the ground."

Lieutenant Fowler's cynicism shocks me, but deep down I know what he says is true. I saw John Tunstall shot in cold blood for daring to challenge Dolan's business monopoly, and the so-called law stood by and did nothing about it. On the other hand, Bill's continuing vendetta isn't right either. Not for the first time, I silently thank the luck that made me a scout for the 10th Cavalry.

"I want you to talk to Frederick Godfroy down at Blazer's Mill and find out what the mood is. If word has reached Victorio about the writ, try and persuade him to stay until I get there."

"I'll try," I say, daunted by the possible responsibility. Will it be up to me to prevent a war?

Deep in thought, I saddle Coronado and set off across the dry hills.

# Blazer's Mill, New Mexico Territory

3 September, 1879

I'm filthy, tired and soaked in sweat as I ride over the last hills separating me from the Tularosa Valley and Blazer's Mill. I'm riding west into the lowering afternoon sun. Behind me my shadow is long and, when I glance back, seems as if it is rushing over the desert floor in a frantic attempt to keep up with me.

I love riding alone through the wild countryside, the sounds of the leather creaking, the bit jangling softly, Coronado's hooves thumping on the ground and occasionally ringing with a sharp metallic sound as they catch a frost-shattered rock.

I've grown to feel equally at home riding across deserts between the bushy cholla cactus and sword-like yucca plants, and winding my way over hills between juniper and pinyon pine trees. I find it hard to remember the lush green of the thick, wet forests where I grew up. That was a childhood world that I have no desire to return to.

There's nothing for me back in Yale anyway. I've had a couple of letters from my mother in the past year. As she said, she has married Sam Billings, sold the stopping house and now helps Sam with the general store. She's happy and I'm glad for her, but Yale isn't my world anymore.

It feels odd coming back to Blazer's Mill, where I spent so many months recovering from my broken leg, but it'll be good to see Godfroy again, and sample Clara's wonderful stew. I just hope I'm ahead of the news about the writ.

I'm so engrossed in my thoughts and the sun is so low in the sky ahead of me that I don't see the man until I'm right next to him. He's standing, completely still, beside a scrub pine. His body's facing over the valley below, but his head is turned toward me. He's a short but powerfully built Apache warrior, dressed in traditional loose leggings and shirt belted with a wide woven belt. He is not wearing a head-band and his long hair falls loosely on either side of his broad face. He appears middle-aged and there are flecks of gray in his hair. His expression is calm and his eyes, deep set above prominent cheekbones, stare at me with interest.

"*Dagot'e*," I say, using a greeting I have heard our Apache scouts use.

A brief flicker of a smile flits across the man's features and he nods but remains silent.

"I am Jim Doolen," I add, patting myself on the chest. "I'm a scout with Lieutenant Fowler at Fort Stanton."

Again the man nods. "I am Bidu-ya," he says simply in a surprisingly soft voice. "I know you."

"What?" I ask, puzzled. I'm convinced I've never met this man before.

"You are Busca. Too-ah-yay-say said you would come."

"You know Wellington? He's here?"

The man obviously does not think my stupid questions deserve an answer. He turns and strides across the small clearing, mounts a pony with an agility I would not have expected of a man his age and rides off down the hill while I am still struggling to understand what just happened.

A burst of firing distracts me and I trot over and look down into the broad valley. A group of five cowboys are trying to lead some twenty ponies along the valley trail. From the trees on the surrounding hills, Apache warriors are attacking them. Some of the attackers are on horseback, others on foot, and they are firing as they run. I'm surprised to see that the attackers are being led by a woman on a black and white piebald pony. Instead of riding straight at the cowboys, she is galloping back and forth organizing the others and trying to reach the trail ahead of the robbers.

The five men on the trail are milling about in confusion, trying to control the horses and firing back wildly. One man appears to take control. He shouts orders, abandons the horses he is leading and rides hard along the trail. The others follow and soon disappear in a dust cloud along the valley.

The Apaches gather the horses and set off back the way the riders had come. The woman sits for a long time watching the dust cloud drift away. A second rider, the man I met up here, Bidu-ya, joins her, and they talk before turning their horses and following the others.

I slowly work my way down to the trail. I have a lot on my mind—the stranger I just met and the woman warrior—but mostly I think about the cowboy who organized the others during the attack. I can't be certain at such a distance, but he looked a lot like Bill.

‡≡

"I knew you would come, Busca." Wellington is sitting beneath a tree near the grave where I saw Brewer and Roberts buried over a year ago.

"How did you know?"

"I dreamed it."

"In the cave with Perdido?"

Wellington smiles. "No, last night in my wickiup."

"Why did you leave your cave?" I ask.

"My story there was done."

"And Perdido's story?" I ask, thinking back to my meeting with the ancient mummified Spanish explorer.

"His story is done as well. I burned him."

"Burned him?"

"He asked me to," Wellington replies matter-of-factly. "He burned very well, with a yellow flame."

Even though Perdido has been dead for centuries, I feel a sense of loss. The way Wellington talked of him, I had almost thought of him as alive. "Why did you come here?"

"I dreamed the end of my story and this is where the end begins."

"Was I in the story?"

"If we are lucky, and if we look hard, we can see the end of our own story. It is not for us to see the end of another's."

"Is Nah-kee-tats-an here?"

"No. He and a few others did not follow Victorio here. They stayed in the mountains of Mexico; that is where *his* story is. But you did not come here for my story or Nah-kee-tats-an's. You are here at the request of the Buffalo Soldiers."

"I am." I look up at the red sunset sky and stand. "I must go and talk to Godfroy."

Wellington snorts derisively. "He is a good man, but he knows nothing." Wellington stands beside me. "I will take you to one who knows."

Before I can ask who, he is striding off toward a collection of grass-covered wickiups farther up the valley. I hurry after him.

"Who are we going to meet?" I manage to ask as we head for a large structure in the center of the group.

"The one you call Victorio," Wellington replies without slowing. I have no time to ask him more before he ducks, pushes aside a skin curtain and enters the domed wickiup.

Inside is surprisingly spacious. The circular floor is at least eight feet across and the height in the middle is almost as much. There is a fire pit in the center of the floor, but it's cold and the smoke hole directly above it lets in the last of the dying daylight. There are two shadowy figures sitting on the opposite side from the entrance, but before I can make out any details, I am distracted by a yell from the figure leaping to his feet to my right.

I just have time to catch a glimpse of a gleam of metal before the man knocks me down, kneels on my chest and holds a long knife to my throat. Even with his face twisted in rage, I recognize my attacker. The ugly, irregular scar on his cheek is from the time I thrust a burning stick at him when he stole my horses not far from here some fifteen months ago. It's the man called Ghost Moon.

A soft, imperious voice from across the floor freezes all action. My attacker never takes his eyes off me or relieves the uncomfortable pressure of the knife blade on my throat, but he enters into an argument with the speaker. I have no idea what is being said, but the calm voice dominates, and the knife is withdrawn. Ghost Moon stands up and stares at me sullenly as I roll over and get to my knees.

I look over at the owner of the voice that saved my life. It's Bidu-ya, the short man I met on the hillside. Beside him sits the striking woman who led the attack on the horse thieves. "Thank you," I say. "Are you Victorio?"

The man nods. "That is what you call me." He indicates the woman. "This is my sister, Lozen." Victorio must have caught my glance at the woman by his side, because he goes on, "Do not underestimate her because she is a woman. Lozen has chosen the warrior's life. She is my right hand, as strong as any man and braver than most, and she is favored by the gods, a true shield to her people."

Victorio's English is very good, which is not surprising, considering all the years he has spent on reservations and negotiating with the army. "Ghost Moon I think you know," he goes on as the scarred man beside me grunts in anger. "Do not fear him. I have said he cannot kill you yet."

The use of *yet* sends a shiver through me, but I resist the temptation to glance over at Ghost Moon. "I am honored to meet you," I say.

Victorio ignores my flattery. "Lozen tells me that the army will come down here tomorrow. Do you know why?"

I'm unsettled both by Victorio's bluntness and by how Lozen could possibly know that Fowler is leading his troop here tomorrow. "They are coming to protect you," I blurt out.

Victorio smiles. "As you saw today, Lozen is perfectly capable of protecting us. Unless you do not mean protection from bands of horse thieves."

"I...I don't know," I stammer, uncomfortable with Victorio's sharpness. I'm not prepared to come here and debate this man, only to ask Godfroy how things are going on the reserve.

Victorio doesn't allow me any time to think. "If not the horse thieves, then perhaps the ranchers who accuse me of murder?"

"You know about that?"

"I have only heard vague rumors. I did not know for certain until you confirmed it just now." I silently curse my stupidity as Victorio continues. "But how can your army protect me against your law? The Buffalo Soldiers can shoot horse thieves because they break the law, but if the sheriff from Lincoln comes here with a piece of paper from a judge ordering my capture or return to San Carlos, then your army must either stand by or help in my arrest."

What Victorio says is true, but before I can think of anything to say, Ghost Moon angrily shouts out a string of Apache.

Victorio ignores him and continues to address me. "Ghost Moon says that we have almost a hundred warriors here and that we will kill any sheriff or soldiers who come to try and send us back to San Carlos. I think he is correct in saying that many of us prefer to die than return to starve in the barren desert in the midst of our enemies, but he underestimates the Buffalo Soldiers, and I do not wish to die here. I will live here in peace if I am allowed to, but I will die for Warm Springs."

Victorio pauses and then says, "Tell me your story, Busca."

"What?" I ask. Just when I think what Victorio is saying is settling into a pattern, he swings off in a different direction. It's disconcerting and keeps me off balance.

"I would hear your story."

Hesitantly at first but gaining confidence, I tell of my adventures since arriving from Canada.

Throughout my monologue, Victorio nods encouragement. When I am done, he says, "Too-ah-yay-say was correct; it is a fine story. And now"—he looks over at the man who attacked me—"Ghost Moon has heard your story as well. It is more difficult to kill a man whose story you have been told."

Ghost Moon stands up abruptly, says something in Apache and storms out of the wickiup. I look at Victorio for a translation, but he simply says, "I expect you need to talk with Godfroy." It is obviously a dismissal, so Wellington and I duck out into the thickening dark.

I look around nervously, half expecting Ghost Moon to lunge at me out of the shadows, but nothing happens as Wellington and I walk back toward Blazer's Mill.

"What did Ghost Moon say before he left?" I ask.

Wellington is silent for a minute. Eventually he starts telling me a story that has nothing to do with my question. "Have you heard of Eskiminzin of the Aravaipa band?"

When I say no, Wellington continues. "The Aravaipas lived north of the cave I shared with Perdido around Camp Grant in the days before it became San Carlos.

33

Eskiminzin struggled for many years to find a peaceful home for his people. Eventually, in the winter of 1871, a Lieutenant Whitman allowed the Aravaipas to settle in a nearby valley. Whitman was a good man and hired Eskiminzin's people to work the land and cut hay for the fort. Eskiminzin was happy; finally his people were at peace and prospering. He became close friends with Whitman and with a rancher called McKinney, who employed many Aravaipas. They spent many evenings talking and smoking together.

"Unfortunately, there were those who did not wish peace or to see the Aravaipas work for the army, as it took money away from them. They raided ranches around Tucson, trying to blame Eskiminzin. When that did not work, they planned murder. Early one morning, before daybreak when most of the men were off hunting, a group of men from Tucson, Americanos and Papagos, who were the Aravaipa's traditional enemies, attacked Eskiminzin's camp."

Wellington hesitates and I wait. Although I cannot see the story having anything to do with the question I asked, I am intrigued.

"It was over in half an hour. The Papagos went through the village stabbing and smashing the skulls of the sleeping women and children. Those who woke in time to flee were shot down by the waiting Americanos, who afterward went through the village finishing off the wounded and setting fire to the wickiups.

"Whitman was at breakfast in Camp Grant when he heard of the attack. He immediately led his soldiers up the valley to see what was going on. He was too late. All he found were the mutilated bodies of over a hundred women and children. Twenty-eight children were also taken back to Tucson as slaves."

"That's awful," I say, thinking that Wellington's silence marks the end of his story. "Were the attackers caught?"

Wellington continues as if I haven't said anything. "Such was the trust the Aravaipas put in Whitman that the survivors, including Eskiminzin who had lost his two wives and six of his children in the massacre, returned from the hills to Fort Grant. Some peace returned, although the wails of mourning filled the valley.

"As time passed, Eskiminzin saw that the children were not returned and those responsible were not being punished. He knew that the attackers had army rifles, so some important people in Tucson must have supplied them. He also knew that Whitman, for all his good intentions, could not protect the Aravaipas. It was only a matter of time before another massacre happened.

"One evening Eskiminzin went to see the rancher McKinney. McKinney welcomed his friend and the pair sat down to supper together. They laughed, talked and smoked. When the meal was done, Eskiminzin pulled his pistol from his belt and shot McKinney in the head."

"Why?" I ask in shock. "McKinney was his friend."

"Eskiminzin walked out of McKinney's ranch house and soon after led his people into the hills away from Camp Grant.

"Later, after starvation forced Eskiminzin to return to the reservation, he was asked the very question you just asked me. He said he had killed McKinney because he knew that there could be no true friendship between the white men and the Aravaipas, and he had to show his people that. He said it is easy to kill an enemy but that killing a friend is difficult."

We walk on in silence for a bit before I say, "That was a horrific story, but what does it have to do with what Ghost Moon said in the wickiup?"

"Ghost Moon is an Aravaipas. He was a mere boy, away hunting with his father when the massacre occurred, but his mother and two sisters died in the valley that morning. Ghost Moon's heart has been filled with hate ever since. As he left the wickiup, he said, 'It is easy to kill an enemy.'"

## 4 September, 1879

"But you and your Buffalo Soldiers cannot protect us against your own law."

Victorio is sitting on the ground outside Blazer's Mill. As in the wickiup, Lozen sits impassively by his side. A number of other warriors, including Wellington and the scowling Ghost Moon, form the rest of a semi-circle facing Lieutenant Fowler, Godfroy, myself, Sergeant Rawlins and several troopers.

I spent the night at Blazer's Mill and enjoyed one of Clara's famous meals, and met Fowler as he rode in around lunchtime today. It's now midafternoon, and the talking between Victorio and Fowler has been going on for almost an hour, a long time in the hot sun.

"That is true," Lieutenant Fowler says. "If the Sheriff comes to arrest you, as the writ says he must, I cannot prevent it."

"Then what use are you and your soldiers?" Ghost Moon interrupts angrily. "All you can do is sit by and watch Bidu-ya cast into prison. If any try to aid him, they will be shot."

Fowler ignores Ghost Moon's outburst and continues talking directly to Victorio. "All I can do is urge you to trust in American justice."

Ghost Moon snorts loudly, but Victorio says calmly, "That is not an easy thing for us. We have been promised many things over the years by many Americans. We were promised the land that the gods gave us at Warm Springs for as long as the mountains stood." Victorio dramatically scans the surrounding hills. "I still see mountains, and yet we are here with our Mescalero brothers at Tularosa and not at Warm Springs. Can you promise, Lieutenant, that when the moon is next full, I will not be in a jail cell in Lincoln and my people back on the desert trail to San Carlos?"

Fowler looks weary and beaten. "I do not have the authority to promise that, but"—he raises his voice as a murmur passes among some of the warriors across from him—"I can promise that my troopers will protect you as long as you stay here and that we will fight beside you if you are attacked."

"As you did yesterday when the cowboys tried to steal our horses." Ghost Moon's voice is heavy with sarcasm. "We do not need your protection."

"I do not wish to become your enemy," Victorio says softly. "Will you fight us if we try to leave?"

"It is my job," Fowler replies.

"Very well then," Victorio says as he stands. The other warriors join him. "If it must be so, we will meet again on the battlefield." Victorio and the others turn and stride off toward their wickiups.

Fowler sighs and stands up. He stretches and regards the surrounding hills thoughtfully. "Sergeant Rawlins," he says eventually, "have the men feed and water the horses and prepare the equipment, we may be riding again sooner than we expected."

"Yes, sir." Rawlins salutes and leads the troopers toward the livery stable.

Fowler returns the salute. "How many are there here in Victorio's band?" he asks Godfroy.

"Between seventy-five and one hundred warriors and their families."

"And how many Mescaleros?"

"At last count, three hundred and twenty-five, half of whom are women and children."

Fowler strokes his chin thoughtfully. "So there are about two hundred and fifty warriors here, and we can probably assume that most will fight if trouble breaks out."

"I would think so," Godfroy agrees.

"And I have thirty troopers here with only the ammunition they carry in their saddlebags."

"It'll be a massacre if Victorio decides to leave and you try to stop him," Godfroy says quietly.

"You may be right," Fowler says. "Thank you, Mr. Godfroy. Walk with me, Jim, while I think."

Godfroy returns to Blazer's Mill, and Fowler and I set off. We walk in silence for some time, following a random route around the settlement. I'm seriously frightened. The prospect of us trying to stop a determined Victorio and his warriors leaving here is a recipe for disaster, but what choice does Fowler have? A series of expressions cross the Lieutenant's features—confusion, worry, anger. Eventually, he stops walking and nods to himself. "I need your advice as a scout. If...When Victorio leaves, where will he go?"

"To Warm Springs," I reply. "He makes no secret of that being his home, a sacred place given to his people by the gods. He knows the land, and if he is going to fight, I think that is where he'll do it."

"I think so too. He'll leave here very soon, possibly tonight, and head west to lose himself in the Black Range, mountains he knows like the back of his hand.

"The cowboys you saw attempting to steal horses yesterday, where will they be headed?"

I think back to the cowboy that reminded me of Bill. "I believe they were Regulators. That means they will probably head east back to the old McSween place and the hills they know."

"I think you're right," Fowler says almost cheerfully, "and I think I'll take your advice."

"What advice?" I ask.

"Why, the advice you have just given me. It is our responsibility to keep the peace on the reservation and protect the Apaches. That peace was broken yesterday by the cowboys. Do you not think it is the army's responsibilities to hunt down those accountable and bring them to justice?"

"I suppose so," I say.

"Excellent, then I shall go and inform Rawlins to have the men ready to leave in one hour. Please go and tell Victorio that we will be heading out after the cowboys in an easterly direction."

Fowler turns on his heel and strides over to the livery stables. I watch him go with a smile on my lips. If Victorio decides to leave tonight, we'll be away in the opposite direction chasing the Regulators. We won't technically be doing anything wrong, and there will be no massacre at Blazer's Mill.

⊹

"Your Lieutenant Fowler is an intelligent man. He has saved many lives today." I'm standing beside the Apache wickiups, talking with Wellington. I have just finished informing Victorio and Lozen that we shall be leaving within the hour to head east in search of the horse thieves. They received the news without comment.

"But how many other lives will be lost when Victorio leaves the reservation and begins raiding?" I ask.

"We cannot control the future," Wellington says. "And if you all stayed, then you would only be the first to die. Victorio would still lead his people to Warm Springs."

"I suppose so. Will you go with him?"

Wellington nods. "It is my destiny."

"Even if it means that we might become enemies?"

"We will never be enemies, Busca. Even if we fight in battles on opposite sides, we shall always be brothers. Our stories are one. It is not our destiny to meet in battle."

"You've dreamed this?"

Wellington smiles. "No. I just know it. But Lieutenant Fowler comes to speak with you. I must go."

I look over to see Fowler walking toward us. "Goodbye, Wellington. I hope we meet once more in happier circumstances."

"I, too, wish that, Busca, but I do not see many happy times in the future. Goodbye."

Wellington walks off and Fowler joins me. "He is your friend?"

"Yes. He was the first decent person I met when I came to this land. The first one who didn't try to trick me, kill me or steal from me. He taught me a lot."

"That's good. Did you tell Victorio what we were planning?"

"I did. He made no comment."

"Good. Now let's get saddled up. We have a long hard ride to Fort Stanton."

"Fort Stanton?" I ask. "I thought we were going searching for the Regulators."

"They have a long start. We'll never find them, but it's good that Victorio thinks that's how we're going to spend our time. He may travel more slowly. If we get to Stanton quickly with the news that he is gone, Colonel Dudley may be able to get a force together in time to catch up with him before he has time to settle into the mountains around Warm Springs."

"You used me to trick him," I say.

"Not entirely. We are heading east and I did save all our lives. Now, let's get moving. We have some long, hard riding ahead of us."

# Fort Stanton, New Mexico Territory

**12 September, 1879**

"I do not wish to be bothered with this matter anymore."

Colonel Nathan Dudley is a thin man with a pompous bearing and a full mustache that seems to weigh his face down. For almost a week now, Lieutenant Fowler has been struggling to persuade Dudley to mount an expedition to attempt to cut off Victorio before he reaches Warm Springs. With every passing day, the chances of achieving anything grow slimmer. "You have no firm evidence, other than the speculations of this scout"—Dudley spits out the word as if it has a bad taste—"that Victorio is headed for Warm Springs. He's probably in Mexico by now. I will not lead my command on a wild-goose chase."

"But if Victorio is headed for Warm Springs, something he has done before every time he has left a reservation, our best chance of recapturing him is before he gets there. He knows the Black Range Mountains as well as we know the layout of this fort. It would take a thousand men and weeks to track him down once he's in there." Fowler is struggling to hide the frustration in his voice. He knows a chance is being missed, in fact has probably been missed, but he feels a responsibility to try and change the stubborn Dudley's mind.

"Then why," Dudley asks with a superior air, "did you not stop him leaving the reservation when you had the chance?"

"As I said in my report, sir, my troop was outnumbered almost ten one by Apache warriors. It would have been a massacre."

"Massacre or not, Lieutenant, you had a duty, and I have my doubts about how well you carried that duty out. If I receive orders from headquarters to move the men to Warm Springs, I shall do so. Until then, I do not wish to hear another word on the matter. Good day."

"Thank you, sir." Fowler forces himself to remain polite to his commanding officer, salutes stiffly and we both leave the office. Outside, he kicks the dirt in frustration. "That man is insufferable," he says bitterly.

"Why does he insist on doing nothing?" I ask as we head across the parade ground.

"Many reasons," Fowler says. "He would obviously rather remain safe and comfortable here than be roughing it on the trail, but there's more to it than just that. I have heard that Susan McSween has brought charges against him."

"What for?"

"Negligence in the death of her husband in Lincoln last year."

I think back to the battle I was caught up in on the streets of Lincoln in July more than a year ago. Dudley wasn't directly responsible for McSween's death—Bill had that burden to carry—but he had been involved that day. The army had been under orders not to interfere in the war between Dolan and McSween, but Dudley had brought troops to town on the pretext of protecting the women and children. What he had in fact done was organize his men so that they supported Dolan and aimed his cannon at McSween's house. I was pretty sure that Bill had been correct when he said that

Dudley was getting a cut of the money from the army contracts that Dolan had a monopoly on.

"Will she win the case?" I ask.

"I doubt it. It's all too murky now, and who will testify? All those who were on McSween's side are either dead or fled. However, it could be seen as a blot on Dudley's record and lead to him being posted to somewhere less comfortable than Fort Stanton."

"So we're going to miss the chance to get Victorio back on the reservation because Dudley wants to stay here and look after his legal concerns."

"I can't speak for Dudley's reasoning, but I do think we've missed a chance. If Victorio is intent on war, it will be much longer and bloodier than it might have been."

We walk in silence until we're interrupted by the arrival of a squad of dust-covered riders. They spot Fowler and rein in before him. The lieutenant in charge is little more than a boy. He dismounts, salutes and hands Fowler a letter. "A message for Colonel Dudley," he says.

"Thank you." Fowler returns the salute. "You're from the 9th at Warm Springs," he adds, looking at the regimental insignia on the saddlebags.

"Yes, sir," the young man replies. "I bring orders for the Colonel to bring a troop down to join us there.

The Black Range is crawling with Apaches. Two days past, they caught E Company in a canyon, killed five troopers and three scouts, stole fifty horses and vanished."

"Victorio?" Fowler asks.

"We think so, sir."

Fowler nods slowly. "I'll see that the colonel gets this message. Jim, find Sergeant Rawlins and tell him we'll be moving out soon."

"I will," I say.

"Lieutenant, have your men see to their horses and get yourselves something to eat." Fowler sets off back toward Dudley's office.

"Yes, sir," the young lieutenant calls after him.

I set off to look for Rawlins. So everything is confirmed—Victorio has left the reservation, made it safely to his beloved Black Range and declared war on the army. I think back to the strong, intelligent man I met at Blazer's Mill, sitting beside his silent fighting sister. Give them warriors filled with as much hatred as Ghost Moon and the war will be long and bloody. Despite what he said, Wellington and I *are* now enemies.

# Near the Black Range,
# New Mexico Territory

**17 September, 1879**

"Bury them and let's move on."

Colonel Dudley's voice rings out across the barren valley bottom. Several soldiers dismount and begin digging ten holes in a long line, while others ride out to retrieve the scattered corpses. The bodies are already bloated in the heat and the exposed skin burned. Anything of value has been stripped from the men.

"Probably miners from the Black Range," Fowler muses as we ride across the sad scene. "That's where they were coming from anyway. Most likely headed for Silver City and thought there would be safety in numbers. I doubt they expected to run into a hundred warriors who saw them as trespassers on sacred land."

We rein in where the valley narrows beside the swollen bodies of six horses. Coronado is skittish near so much death. Three vultures, their heads bloody and their movements sluggish from gorging, waddle a short distance away from one of the carcasses, cawing protest at our interruption of their meal. There is only one human body here, trapped beneath one of the horses. The vultures have been here as well and I don't look too closely.

"This is where it began," Fowler says, scanning the surrounding ground to read the story of the battle. "They hid behind those rocks and scrub and opened fire as the miners passed. Aimed for the horses. Once they were dead or wounded, the warriors could pick off the men at leisure." He looks back the way we have come. Five bodies are strewn singly along the trail. All have been shot. Farthest away lie the last four, broken arrow shafts standing from chests and backs.

"My guess is that mounted warriors came out of that canyon to the left and cut off the running men's retreat. Those four knew they were finished, so they stopped. Probably ran out of ammunition. The Apaches got close enough to finish them off with bows to save bullets."

We stare silently at the grisly scene. I try to imagine what it must have been like for the last four, using their final shots and standing together, knowing they were doomed. Despite the heat, I shiver.

"Looks like Victorio headed back into the mountains up ahead. I sure hope Dudley isn't aiming to take us in there after him."

"What else can we do?"

"Wait. Guard all the water holes and trails out of the mountains. Victorio will have to come down from there to raid and get supplies sooner or later. Then we can fight him on our terms. If we go in there, it's his country and he can choose where to fight. We would have as little chance as these miners."

Sergeant Rawlins and another man arrive and begin hauling the miner's body out from under the horse. Fowler and I trot back down the valley to where the bodies are being laid out beside the deepening graves.

This ambush reminds me of the time I came across the site where Nah-kee-tats-an's party had been attacked by scalp hunters. That time it had been white men attacking Apaches; this time it was Apaches attacking white men, but the end was the same: bodies strewn among the rocks and cactus. In a war it didn't seem to matter whose side you were on. The result was death.

# Las Animas Canyon, Warm Springs, New Mexico Territory

**Morning, 18 September, 1879**

"They're cornered up this canyon. We have them where we want them; all we need to do is go and get them."

It's dawn and Colonel Dudley is standing in his stirrups addressing us and the four troops of the 9th Cavalry that we met up with yesterday. We're mounted and ready to go, scattered over a flat area at the mouth of Las Animas Canyon, which leads straight into the heart of the Black Range. "The 10th with Companies A and B of the 9th will proceed up the canyon. I will wait here in reserve with Companies C and D. Advance."

Amid jangling equipment, shouted orders and a growing cloud of dust, about seventy-five of us set off in loose order up the valley. I'm riding beside Lieutenant Fowler and hear him mutter, "Not only is he sending us into the lion's mouth, but he's also split his force. He's another Custer." I try not to think too hard about what that might mean. Fowler turns to Sergeant Rawlins and the men following us. "Keep close to the canyon wall and in among as much cover as you can find."

After about half a mile, the walls of the canyon move in toward us, forcing most of the troops into single file in the center. The narrow floor is rugged and boulder-strewn, and the walls looming over us are steep. Isolated spires of rock look like tall sentinels watching our puny force move deeper into the mountains. Fowler and I are to one side, close under the right-hand canyon wall, picking our way cautiously through some mesquite trees.

Up ahead, a side canyon joins. A wide, flat outcrop protects its mouth.

"Keep your eyes peeled," Fowler shouts. Then he continues more quietly, "Twenty men on that flat rock could keep us pinned here all day."

As if by magic, figures appear on the rock and along the ridgeline across from us. The first volley kills half of the horses out on the canyon floor. The screams of horses, yelled orders and gunshots echo against the rock walls. The forelegs of Fowler's horse buckle, throwing him over the neck. Coronado holds steady, and I slide from the saddle to join Fowler on the ground. A bullet thuds into a tree trunk above my head. I lead Coronado even closer to the canyon wall, into the thickest underbrush I can find. Fowler, Sergeant Rawlins and a trooper are crouching behind a large rock on the edge of the trees. The trooper is bleeding from a bullet wound in his right thigh and is sitting, cursing steadily.

The initial chaos is calming and the rate of fire from the ridge is lessening as troopers manage to find cover, some behind the bodies of their horses, others behind the rocks or scrub trees. There are bodies of horses everywhere, some still, some trying to rise and others twitching pitifully. Several horses stand around, riderless, stamping nervously. I can't see the bodies of any troopers. The Apaches were obviously going for the horses with the first volley, but I have no idea how many are wounded like the man beside Rawlins.

"Return fire." I hear a voice shouting orders.

Rawlins pops his head over the rock and fires a shot at the ridgeline. "Nothing to shoot at but rocks and sky," he says. "How you doing, Sam?" he asks his companion.

"Okay," the wounded man replies through gritted teeth. "The bone ain't broke and the bleeding's easing if I keep my kerchief on it, but it hurts like the devil."

"Are you okay, Jim?" Fowler shouts over to me.

"I am."

"And your horse?"

"Coronado's fine," I say. "The trees are sheltering us."

"Good," Fowler says. "Now listen carefully. I want you to ride back down the canyon and find Dudley and the other two companies. We're helpless here without our horses. We can't retreat and we can't attack up these steep walls against such heavy rifle fire. Victorio can sit up there all day and pick us off at his leisure.

"Tell the colonel what happened and say that I'm requesting he put men up on the ridgeline back down the canyon. If they can work up to positions that overlook Victorio's, we can drive them off. Keep low in the saddle and ride as hard as you can. Rawlins and I'll give you what covering fire we can."

"Yes, sir," I acknowledge. I climb back into the saddle and lie along Coronado's neck. At first, I can work my way through the trees without being exposed to the riflemen on the ridge, but the trees soon thin out at the edge of a rock fall.

"Okay," I whisper in Coronado's ear, "now we have to go out in the open. They'll be surprised to begin with, so that'll give us a start. Go as fast as you can, but watch where you put your hooves. A broken leg will finish us both. Let's go."

We burst from the trees and veer wildly down the canyon. I can do little more than hold on for dear life, but Coronado is magnificent. The ground is littered with rocks, but he never puts a hoof wrong. Before I am even aware that people are firing at us, we are around the first corner and safe.

I slow Coronado down and sit up in the saddle, scanning the ridgeline on both sides. It's bare. I feel a huge rush of relief. I've made it, now all I have to do is find Dudley and pass on Lieutenant Fowler's message. It doesn't take long. Dudley and the two companies of the 9th have heard the firing and are already heading up the canyon.

Dudley rides forward when he sees me coming. "Who are you?" he asks curtly.

"I'm Lieutenant Fowler's scout," I say. "The lieutenant says—" I begin, but Dudley cuts me off.

"Oh yes, the Regulator who was bushwhacked by the Indians at Blazer's Mill. What's happening up ahead? Have you been bushwhacked again?"

"Yes. No. I mean…" I stammer, unsettled by the excitement and by Dudley's abrupt manner. "We were ambushed. Most of the horses are dead and we're pinned down."

"Seventy-five men pinned down? There must be a lot of Indians up there."

"They're up on the ridge above us. The canyon's narrow and the walls are steep. Lieutenant Fowler suggests that you—"

Anger flashes across Dudley's thin face. "Lieutenant Fowler presumes to suggest what I should do! That man holds too high a regard for these Indians by far." Dudley turns in his saddle and addresses the men behind him. "Arms at the ready. Open order. Advance."

I sit stunned as the troopers ride past me. "Wait," I shout, but Dudley ignores me. There's nothing for me to do but follow along.

My first reaction when we reach the scene of the fight is that Victorio has left. Silence reigns. Dudley and his men ride boldly up the middle of the canyon. Other troopers emerge from behind rocks. All of a sudden, all hell breaks loose. Concentrated rifle fire sweeps the floor of the canyon. Horses drop, men shout and scurry back to cover. It's a hideous repeat of the first ambush.

I swing Coronado off into the trees and dismount. Leaving him where the trees are thickest, I work my way back to Lieutenant Fowler's rock. Fowler and the Rawlins are still there, firing up at the ridgeline. Dudley's companies have joined the rest behind rocks and trees, and those horses not dropped by the rifle fire are galloping back down the canyon in disorder.

"Idiot," Fowler shouts as the firing dies away to sporadic shots. I don't know whether he's referring to Dudley or me.

"I tried to tell him about the ridgeline, but he wouldn't listen," I say.

"And now everyone's trapped," he says bitterly.

"Lieutenant Day," Dudley shouts from somewhere in the middle of the canyon. "Take the men nearest you and climb the canyon wall ahead. Clear that ridgeline."

"Yes, sir," a voice replies from farther ahead. I see movement among the rocks and hear commands shouted back and forth. Eventually, about fifteen men break from cover and head for the tress farther up the canyon. There's a burst of firing, but I don't see anyone fall.

While Day and the others are out of sight in the trees, the firing dies away. The slope above the trees is steep and bare, and I have the sense that everyone is waiting to see what happens when the men reach it.

Oddly, nothing happens as Day and the others reappear and begin toiling over the open ground. The men try to use whatever pitiful cover the loose rocks afford, but they are brutally exposed. They move slowly, frequently almost crawling. I wonder why the Apaches don't open fire on the exposed men.

The scattered shots ring out as the leading man reaches the ridgeline. He slumps backward and lies still. Two other figures drop and roll a short way down the slope. The rest scatter into whatever cover they can find. Now I realize why the Apaches waited—they have caused casualties and trapped the rest of Day's men in an exposed position with no hope of going either forward or back.

### Afternoon, 18 September, 1879

Sporadic firing goes on for several hours. Nothing changes except that several soldiers cry out in pain as they are wounded, and our ammunition runs low.

The wounded trooper beside Fowler alternately groans and curses softly.

"How many bullets do you have left?" Fowler asks Sergeant Rawlins, who has been steadily firing at the ridgeline all morning.

"I'm out, sir," Rawlins replies. "Been using Sam's for the past hour. Got six shots left."

"And I'll wager you've killed no Apaches."

Rawlins hesitates. "We're keeping their heads down," he says.

"That's true enough," Fowler says, "but hold your fire. You'll need all of those cartridges come dusk and we retreat."

"Retreat?" I blurt out.

"Day's trapped up on the ridge, and we're trapped down here and running out of ammunition. Do you have a better idea?"

I don't. I just hadn't thought that far ahead. Fowler is beginning to explain how the retreat will be carried out when movement out in the canyon distracts me. Several troopers are working their way closer from rock to rock. Eventually about thirty are clustered in the trees around me.

An officer flops down beside Fowler. "Lieutenant Bob Emmet," he says, holding out a hand.

"George Fowler," Fowler replies, returning the handshake.

"Colonel Dudley has ordered me to collect all the able-bodied men I can and lead them up that side canyon behind you. There's a second ridgeline behind the Apaches. If we can take that, we outflank them." Fowler and I both instinctively look up toward the canyon Emmet has mentioned. We can't see it from the trees, but I remember it as being narrow and very steep.

"Well then, I guess that's what we'll have to do," Fowler says. "You stay here," he orders Rawlins. "Take care of the wounded man and don't shoot unless you're sure of a target."

"Yes, sir," Rawlins replies, but he doesn't look happy at being left behind.

"Come on, Jim," Fowler adds. "Let's go with Lieutenant Emmet and win a couple of medals."

Moving through the trees is fairly safe, but my heart sinks when we come out into the open at the mouth of the narrow side canyon. There's no cover for a long way, and the ground is rough and brutally steep. The one advantage is that we are passing beneath the end of the ridge that Victorio's men occupy so few of them can fire down on us. The difficulty will come when we begin to climb onto the far ridge. The top is partially treed with scrub oak, but the slope leading to it is bare.

In the heat of the afternoon the going is cruel, and I'm soaked in sweat even before we get to the steepest part of the climb. My legs hurt with every step, and I am concentrating on simply putting one foot in front of the other. I'm so wrapped up in my own pain that I don't even notice we are being fired on until the man beside me curses and stumbles against me. I think he has tripped until I see the blood seeping between the fingers clutching his right arm.

"I'm hit," he says stupidly.

"You can't stay here," I say. "It's only your arm. You can still climb. Keep going. You'll be safer in the trees."

Without complaint, the man does as I've told him and keeps climbing. I help him over the roughest bits. Some men are in the trees now, and I'm almost there.

The wounded trooper beside me suddenly coughs and falls forward. "Come on," I gasp. "We're nearly there." I reach down and pull his unwounded arm. "Get up," I say, angry that he's given up and forced me to slow down.

The man's head flops comically to the side. His eyes are wide-open, staring at nothing. Blood is seeping out through his hair. Awkwardly, I drag him the last few feet into the trees and collapse, panting like a sick dog. Every breath hurts, but I gradually calm down. "He's dead." I look up to see Fowler kneeling beside me.

"I know."

"That's two we lost on the climb." Fowler nods back to the open. A trooper is out in the open, hunched over beside a large rock. He could be resting except for the large bloodstain across his back.

"Are we going to leave him out there?" I ask.

"Do you want to go back to get him? We'll take the bodies down when we go. Right now we need to get to the other end of the ridge so we can see what we're firing at."

Slowly we work our way through the trees. The oaks are close, but every time we cross an open area, firing opens up from the next ridge and bullets whistle over our heads or thud into tree trunks. I don't see anyone hit and I'm beginning to think we might succeed when a long arrow appears almost magically out of the shoulder of the man ahead of me. He drops to his knees, clawing uselessly at the feathered shaft.

I look around but see nothing to suggest where the arrow came from. The trees are thick here, and there is heavy underbrush below them, so it's hard to see more than a few yards. I turn my head to ask Lieutenant Fowler what to do. I hear the arrow swish past my ear and feel the air ruffle my hair. I look back in time to see movement in the underbrush about sixty feet ahead of me. Fowler's seen it too. He draws his revolver and rushes forward.

In less time than it takes to understand what is happening, a warrior rises from the underbrush. His scarred face is painted, half in blood red and half in midnight black. Branches and oak leaves are tied in his hair and onto his shirt. He looses off a single arrow and vanishes between the trees.

The arrow catches Fowler in the left shoulder, and I watch in horror as the point juts out of his back. He is on the ground by the time I reach him, lying on his right side, his face a mask of pain.

"Are you all right?" I ask.

Fowler sucks air noisily through his teeth. "Never better," he says with an attempt at a smile. "But I think we should get this arrow out, don't you?"

"How?"

"First, break off the barbed point as close to my back as possible."

I examine the bloodstained point. It's made of iron and is quite narrow, but there's no doubt it would make a mess of Fowler's shoulder if I tried to pull it back through from the front. The lieutenant's right, it has to be broken off.

The arrow entered below Fowler's collarbone and sticks out about four inches from the muscle that leads up to his neck. I grip the shaft with my left hand, tight up against Fowler's back and take the rest of it in my right. I try to break it, but all that happens is the shaft moves and Fowler gasps in pain.

"Don't push it around," he says. "Just grip as hard as you can and snap it."

I tighten my grip, close my eyes and snap the shaft. The arrowhead slices open the soft flesh of my palm, and Fowler grunts loudly, but the arrow is broken and only about an inch and a half now stick out of my friend's back.

Fowler rolls onto his back and looks up at me. Some two feet of shaft sticks up from his shoulder, ending in three brown-flecked turkey feathers. "Now," he says firmly, "put your foot on my chest, grip the arrow and pull it out in one movement. Pull hard; I don't want you to have to do it twice."

"Okay," I say. I place my right foot on Fowler's chest, grasp the arrow shaft just below the turkey feathers, take a deep breath and pull. The arrow comes out surprisingly smoothly, and I stumble back as Fowler cries out in pain.

I throw the arrow away and kneel beside Fowler. He's breathing heavily and pressing his right hand hard over the wound. "Thank you." He lifts his hand and squints down at his shoulder. There's a red patch on his uniform, but it's not very big. "It doesn't appear to be bleeding too badly. Have a look at the back."

"It looks about the same," I say. "Some blood soaking into your jacket, but not too much."

"Good, now you get on with the others."

Only now do I notice that soldiers are working their way around us through the trees and there is scattered firing from up ahead. "Will you be all right?" I ask.

"If I don't try to get up and start dancing," Fowler says. "You get on, just don't forget to collect me on the way back down."

I nod and continue through the trees, relieved that Fowler will be all right and that he took the arrow that I think Ghost Moon intended for me.

⇥

We're as trapped as Day at the head of the valley and the others on the valley floor. We've cleared the oak grove on the ridge, but there's open ground farther on that we need to cross to finish the job, and warriors are clustered among the rocks on the heights above us. Their fire forces us back into the trees every time we try to move forward.

I wander about in a daze, obeying orders when given them and worrying about Fowler's wound. I also wonder vaguely if Wellington is somewhere on this ridge. What had seemed to be a straightforward life is suddenly becoming more complicated.

As dusk begins to fall, word is passed along that we are to retreat back down to the canyon floor. I'm heading back through the trees to collect Fowler when I meet Lieutenant Emmet and five troopers. They're heading in the opposite direction.

"I'm not obeying Dudley's order," he says when he draws level with me. "These five men and I are forming a rearguard to try and get the Apaches to keep their heads down while the rest cross that open slope on the way down. You're a civilian and not under my command, so I can't order you, but we could use an extra rifle."

"I have to help Lieutenant Fowler down," I say.

"Two troopers are already helping him. You would be more useful distracting the Apaches while they cross the open ground."

"Okay," I say, turning to follow him.

We crawl unseen into positions behind rocks past the tree line where we can fire on the ridge opposite. As soon as firing begins from the opposite ridge, we open up. I haven't fired a shot yet today, so I have plenty ammunition and fire away blindly at the dark slope. Fire's returned but it's wild. When we are all out of ammunition, Emmet pulls us back.

The way down in the semi-dark is hard and slow, but at least no one can see us. Back in the main canyon we meet up with the rest of Emmet's command. As Emmet organizes us, we are joined by Day and his men. He, too, disobeyed Dudley to stay on the ridge, in his case to rescue one of his wounded troopers.

I go and find Coronado, who is still waiting patiently where I left him. I lead him over and help Fowler onto his back. The other wounded men have found mounts, and without interference from the Apaches, we make our way slowly down Las Animas Canyon to where Dudley is setting up camp on the plain. As soon as we enter the guarded perimeter, Dudley strides angrily forward to meet us. "Day, Emmet, where have you been?"

Both officers begin to explain why they stayed behind, but Dudley interrupts them. "You disobeyed a direct order from your superior officer. I fully intend to bring charges and have you both court-martialed."

I expect the two lieutenants to protest, but they simply say, "Yes, sir," and go about settling their men and posting guards. I lead Coronado over to where the surgeon is tending to the wounded and drop Fowler off. He thanks me again for removing the arrow, and I take Coronado over to the horse lines, unsaddle him, brush him down, and feed and water him. Fighting waves of exhaustion, I wander over to where some troopers are digging eight graves for the men we have lost today. The bodies lie beside them, wrapped in saddle blankets. I stand staring down for a long time, thinking what a mess today has been. A mess for us, but not Victorio—for him it's another victory.

Eventually I become aware of a presence beside me. It's Lieutenant Emmet. "Thank you for your help on the ridge," he says.

I nod acknowledgment.

"It's always hard to lose a man," he adds, looking down at the bodies.

"Will you be court-martialed for disobeying orders?" I ask.

"I doubt it. Dudley's all bluster. Besides, I've heard that he's to be replaced. Something to do with a woman placing charges against him over in Lincoln."

"Mrs. McSween," I say. "Her husband was killed in the battle in Lincoln, and she blames Dudley for it."

"Was he to blame?"

"I don't know. Dudley certainly favored the side that killed McSween."

"Then he is to blame," Emmet says. "The only way the army can become involved in civilian matters is in order to protect the innocent, and then we must protect everyone, regardless of personal prejudice."

"I suppose so." I'm not particularly interested. Exhaustion is sweeping over me. I say goodbye and move through the camp until I find Rawlins and the others. I explain what happened. Overcome by emotion and fatigue, I huddle by the nearest fire and fall into a deathlike sleep.

# Chihuahua City, Mexico

21 October, 1880

The wrench of coming back to the present is like a physical blow, and I sit in silence for a long time, dazed and staring at the street in front of me. The bench feels hard beneath me; the edge digs painfully into my thighs as I lean forward. The cool of the early morning has given way to the inevitable desert heat of noon.

"You were far away," Santiago says eventually.

I nod agreement and shift uncomfortably on the bench.

"Perhaps we should move inside," Santiago suggests. Again I nod and we stand. My limbs ache from being stationary for so long, but Santiago is worse. It takes him quite some time to straighten up and stretch out his back and legs. I notice that he suddenly looks much older. His skin has a grayish color and his breathing is shallow and rasping. Nevertheless, he refuses my offer of help and shrugs off his discomfort as the mere consequences of age. Slowly we move inside to the hotel lounge.

It takes a moment for my eyes to adjust to the gloom. The window shades are drawn to keep out the sun, and no lights are on. The walls are paneled in dark wood up to waist height and papered above in a faded red flowery design. The ceiling is pressed tin, painted white, and the wood floor is partly covered by a dark, intricately patterned rug. There's a large empty fireplace surmounted by a heavy oak mantle set in one wall. The only other furniture is a worn sideboard, a few straggling plants in bright Mexican pots, a red sofa pushed to one side, a low wooden table and two deep, leather armchairs. The room is empty at this time of day, and Santiago and I each take an armchair.

"You are a good storyteller," Santiago says after we have settled and ordered a pitcher of cool water and two glasses. "I was transported by your telling."

"Thank you," I say, sipping the refreshing water. "I almost felt that I was back there in Las Animas Canyon. I could hear the rifle shots and smell the sage and pine."

"Your Colonel Dudley did not seem to have made the best decisions in the battle."

"He didn't, but his involvement was at an end. Dudley moved off to another command, although Lieutenant Fowler's troop remained attached to the 9th Cavalry under Major Morrow."

"How did Lieutenant Fowler's wound heal?"

"Well. The arrow missed anything vital and there was no infection, so, in only a few days, he was back with us, although his arm was in a sling for a time longer. It must have been hard for him as Morrow worked us relentlessly. He believed that the only way to defeat Victorio and force him back onto the reservation was to wear him down, allow him no chance to rest or resupply. As a result, we spent most of September and October last year in the saddle, riding hard from one reported sighting to another. It was frustrating, tiring work because there was never anyone there to fight when we arrived, but I suppose it was even harder on Victorio's band because, late in October, he left his beloved Black Range and fled south into Mexico."

Santiago nodded as if he knew this part of the story. "The American army was not allowed to pursue him across the border."

"That's true, but Morrow was a driven man. We broke the rules and rode across the Rio Grande River after Victorio. It was a mistake. The country was brutal, and the eighty troopers who accompanied Morrow were soon suffering horrors for want of water. The horses were breaking down and we had few supplies, but we kept going, pushing Victorio as hard as we could.

"On October 27, I was riding ahead, searching for the Corralitos River, where we hoped to find water. We had each brought two horses with us and I was riding my spare, Alita, to give Coronado a rest. I was passing a range of low hills when I spotted some dust in a wide canyon. I was heading over to investigate when five Apache warriors appeared round the edge of a low bluff. I guess it was a hunting party, but as soon as they spotted me, they headed fast in my direction. I turned to run, but Alita was slow.

"I felt her shudder when the first bullet hit her right rear haunch. She kept going gamely, but the second shot caught her in the chest. I think it hit her heart because she went down instantly, throwing me forward over her neck. I rolled and scrambled back behind Alita's body and dragged my revolver out of its holster. The revolver was not the ideal weapon at that range, but Alita had fallen on my carbine strapped beside the saddle.

"My first shot was a fluke. I reached over Alita's body and fired at the charging warriors. I had little hope of hitting anything, but my bullet struck the lead warrior square in the chest and catapulted him backward off his pony. His companions reined in and gathered round the fallen man.

"I was in the middle of an open plain with nowhere to hide. As long as I lay where I was, I was protected by the body of my dead horse, but I didn't have much ammunition and couldn't count on the luck of that first shot being repeated. However, I was prepared to sell my life as expensively as possible when the remaining warriors renewed their attack. To my surprise and great relief, they didn't, simply loading their colleague onto his horse and riding off toward the distant hills.

"I waited until they were well away before getting up and hauling the saddle off Alita. I set off walking, frequently looking over my shoulder for signs of pursuit, but there were none. Toward evening, I was found by a squad of troopers out searching for water and taken back to the camp."

"You were lucky," Santiago comments.

"It seemed so at the time," I say sadly, "but I was not."

"It is difficult to lose a horse," Santiago says, thinking I meant the bad luck was the death of Alita. "She was the second called Alita that you lost, was she not?"

"She was," I agree, thinking back to the first horse I had bought in San Diego, a small pony that had brought me into this land and paid for it with her life. I decide not to clarify why I knew that incident was unlucky. Santiago would discover for himself what I meant later in the story.

"The next morning Morrow led us on an attack on the camp I had seen the dust from in the canyon. The fighting was hard, but the warriors knew we were coming and had built stone breastworks on the canyon walls, and try as we might, we couldn't dislodge them. That night, with the horses and troopers at the limits of their endurance, we retreated to find water. Morrow wanted to renew the attack the next day, but it was obvious to everyone that so many horses were close to death that if we did, we would soon be on foot and at Victorio's mercy. We retreated back across the Rio Grande River."

"I heard of that excursion," Santiago says. "It caused quite a fuss among some people here. How dare Americans cross our border without permission? However, I have a brief story of my own that I can add to your experiences here, if you would do me the honor of listening."

"I should very much like to hear your story," I say.

"Excellent. But first I suggest that we order some tortillas. All this riding and fighting has given me an appetite."

I smile and agree. A break will be good, as will listening rather than telling for a while.

"Many of the local people did not share the government's view of the American army," Santiago explains as we work our way through a large plate of tortillas and beans. The food seems to be helping him, and he is looking healthier and more lively than he did only a few hours ago. "Do not take me wrong, we had little love for the Americanos. We had fought them too much recently, but the Apaches were a more ancient enemy, and anyone who fights beside you against your worst enemy is a friend. I think we would have liked to see the border open so that Victorio could not seek refuge on whichever side of the river seemed safest."

"After we crossed back, Major Morrow kept a close watch on as many crossing places as he could, hoping to catch Victorio next time he came north," I say.

"But he did not go north," Santiago says. "He went west, into the Sierra de la Candelaria. Word of your defeat at the Corralitos River spread quickly and with it spread fear. That fear turned to terror when Mescalero raiding parties began passing through the country around Esqueda on their way to join Victorio. Several rancheros nearby were attacked and cattle and horses stolen, and many people moved into the towns for protection."

"Is that why you came to Chihuahua?" I ask.

"No." Santiago shakes his head sadly. "I could not leave Esqueda. Maria was not well at this time. She had taken to wandering off into the desert in the middle of the night, convinced that she was on her way to the Governor's Ball in Monterey. It was a difficult time."

Santiago sits and stares at the tortillas, his hand halfway to his mouth. I can think of nothing to say. What must it be like, helplessly watching someone you have loved all your life go slowly insane before your eyes?

Santiago starts as if suddenly remembering where he is. "But the story I wish to tell you happened to the south of Esqueda. The people of the town of Carizal in the Sierra de la Candelaria decided to do something about the local raids.

"The *alcalde*, the mayor, of Carizal was a city man who had no respect for the Apaches. He persuaded the townspeople that the raiders would flee at the first sign of force. He talked a local figure, the *herrero*…I do not know in English, the man who works iron."

"The blacksmith," I say.

"Yes. Yes. The blacksmith. The mayor persuaded the blacksmith to lead fourteen men into the mountains on the trail of Victorio. When they did not return after a few days, the mayor himself led a party of thirty-five, almost all the able-bodied men left in the town, in a search for them.

"They found the blacksmith's party where the trail passes through a narrow canyon. The bodies were mostly clustered along the trail, but a few men had run into the rocks to attempt to fight back.

"As the relief party gathered the bodies for burial, Apache warriors hidden up in the canyon walls opened fire on them. The second fight in the canyon was longer and harder than the first, but the result was the same. The mayor and all the men with him died, mostly alone, trying to hide among the rocks when their ammunition ran out."

"Fifty men dead?" I ask in shock.

"Yes, fifty," Santiago replies. "Every male from the town who was not a child or an old man. Carizal became a community of weeping women and children."

We sit in silence, thinking. I cannot visualize either the horror of those men scrambling around the canyon seeking a nonexistent safety as they are hunted by the warriors, or the tragedy of the families left without husbands, brothers and sons.

"It's horrific," I say eventually, "but what does it have to do with my story?"

"Several days after the tragedy, an army patrol on the way to Chihuahua came through Carizal. They went to the canyon and buried the bodies. An officer with the patrol was so moved that he swore on the heads of the widows and orphans of Carizal that he would avenge their loss. The officer was Colonel Joaquin Terrazas."

My mind jumps back to the arrogant officer that the boy persuaded to let me go. "The man who captured us and brought us to Chihuahua City."

"The same. So you see, James Doolen, although you did not know it, the final chapter in your story began in that canyon outside Carizal."

Everything is linked—the places I have been, the people I have met and the stories they have told are all part of some puzzle so vast that the whole picture can never be seen.

Santiago sits quietly and watches me as I think through all I have heard. His story is told. It's time for me to go on with mine, but it's not easy. I am sorely tempted to tell stories of that winter and spring, how Victorio led his warriors back to his beloved Warm Springs and how Major Morrow led us back and forth across New Mexico Territory, across the Black Range and the White Sands desert, always one step behind Victorio.

I am tempted to tell Santiago of the dozen or so times we were within an ace of capturing the Apaches, but how, each time, the warriors disappeared into the hills like smoke and we were left scouring empty canyons and ridges and tending our wounded and counting our dead.

I am tempted to tell him countless tragic tales of burned-out ranches surrounded by the bodies of families and destroyed mines with the miners' bodies lying out in the sun nearby. How while we were discovering one tragedy, another was happening twenty miles away in a different direction. How Victorio, with Lozen at his side, won every engagement there was.

I could tell Santiago and it would take days to say it all, but it isn't the story he wants to hear or that I need to tell. I have to jump that spring and move to West Texas a mere two months ago.

The 10th Cavalry was back in Texas, and there was a new policy. Instead of Morrow's idea of chasing Victorio, Colonel Benjamin Grierson had a new plan. The one thing everyone needs in this land on a regular basis is water, and there are only a few places where a party of any size can find enough for themselves and their stock. Grierson realized that and, instead of trying to go and find Victorio, stationed men at each waterhole near the border with Mexico and waited for Victorio to come to him. He did, at Quitman Canyon and Rattlesnake Springs. Short, sharp engagements were fought, and both times Victorio was driven away from water.

These were the first victories for the 10th Cavalry in the whole long war, and Victorio realized immediately how important they were. He turned back for the safety of Mexico, and Lieutenant Fowler's troop was ordered to try and cut off his escape, to delay him crossing the Rio Grande River until the bulk of Grierson's forces could catch him. We rode hard and almost succeeded.

I look at Santiago watching me expectantly, take a deep breath and, once more, travel back in time.

# The Rio Grande River, Texas

**Early afternoon, 9 August, 1880**

"Are there any signs of Victorio having crossed yet?" Lieutenant Fowler asks before I have a chance to report on my scouting along the banks of the Rio Grande.

"A small party, maybe twenty horses, crossed the river on the other side of those hills." I nod to the southeast at the dry, rugged hills that sweep down almost to the river's edge. They end in cliffs that loom over the narrow tree-lined banks of the river. "I doubt if anyone would try and cross from the hills; the cliffs are steep and the river's narrow and fast-flowing.

I think we're here ahead of anyone. They'll probably try and cross right about where we are now."

Fowler scans the river before us. The low brown hills we have recently ridden over end abruptly in a meandering ribbon of bright green trees that wrap the sluggish, brown snake of water along its entire length. Immediately before us the river is wide, about three hundred feet and broken by several sandbars. "So, if we haven't missed them completely, some will try to cross here. I've placed Sergeant Rawlins and five men in the rocks at the edge of those hills, where they can fire down along the length of the river. The rest I've placed among the trees or in whatever rock outcrops offer cover. There aren't enough of us to defeat any kind of sizeable force, but they won't know how many we are, so my hope is they will assume we are more than we are and turn back from the river. That should catch them nicely between us and Grierson.

"You and I will take a position among the rocks on that knoll there." Fowler points to a low boulder-covered hillock standing alone some way in front of the trees. "We'll see anyone approaching a long way off and have plenty of time to return to the trees to organize the men once we know what we face."

We ride over to the hill, tether Coronado and Fowler's horse out of sight between two large boulders and scramble to the top. Fowler's right: from where we lie, we have panoramic views of the surrounding countryside. No one attempting to cross the river here will be able to get within a mile or so without being spotted.

We lie and watch as the day progresses and the horizon shimmers in a heat haze. As I lie beside one of my friends, half of me is hoping that, as on so many occasions before, we are wasting our time. Sooner or later, I am bound to end up on the opposite side from my other friends, Wellington or Nah-kee-tats-an. I don't want to have to make the decisions that that may lead to.

I'm watching a dark green lizard bask on a rock in front of me when Lieutenant Fowler touches my arm. He points at the horizon over to our right. I squint against the glare but soon notice a rising cloud of dust. I stare until I can see the dark figures below the cloud. I estimate around twenty horsemen.

Fowler opens and closes his fist four times, twenty. I nod. Fowler pushes himself back from the edge, scaring the lizard, which scuttles off into a dark crevice. He begins to stand up. I am kneeling when the arrow catches Fowler full in the throat, ripping out one side in a spray of blood. With an odd gurgling sigh, he collapses beside me, his eyes blinking rapidly and a large pool of blood forming frighteningly fast beside his head.

The shock releases me and I have time to reach for my revolver before the back of my head explodes in pain and the bright landscape before me shatters into a thousand diamond-bright shards. My last memory is of falling over my friend's body.

# The Rio Grande River, Mexico

**Evening, 9 August, 1880**

The cold water splashing on my face wakes me. It takes me a minute to realize that my head is hanging upside down and that the water is splashing up at me. A larger wave forces water into my mouth and up my nose, causing me to choke and pull my head up. Pain sears through my skull, but I force myself to hold my head out of the water.

As full awareness returns, I understand that I am draped across Coronado's saddle, my arms and legs tied together under his belly. I sense other horses splashing nearby, but then I have to concentrate on keeping my head above the water. Fortunately, Coronado doesn't have to swim, and we are soon trotting over a sandy shore into a stand of trees.

A knife flashes, and I slide off Coronado and fall painfully to the ground. Hands grab me roughly, drag me over to a tree and tie my wrists behind me around the trunk. Still groggy and confused from the blow to my head, I look around and try to make sense of what is happening.

I am at one edge of a clearing in the trees. About twenty Apache warriors are busy around me, tending to horses, building fires and butchering a deer. Wellington is standing to one side gazing at me. Ghost Moon is beside him, his face filled with hate.

"Where am I?" I slur. My tongue feels too big for my mouth.

"Mexico," Wellington replies simply.

"If you were mine," Ghost Moon snarls, "your body would be lying beside that of your friend on the hill where we found you."

"Why am I not dead?" I ask as I strive to get my befuddled brain to work properly.

"Because, Busca, you do not belong to Ghost Moon," Wellington says. "You belong to me."

"Belong to you?"

"You are my son, Busca."

"Son?" My questions aren't making anything clearer.

"In place of the son you killed."

"Killed? What do you mean? I never killed your son."

Wellington looks at me sadly. "Last year, by the Corralitos River a scout for the army was surprised by a hunting party of warriors. His horse was killed and he lay behind it as the warriors charged. The scout fired off one shot from his revolver. Whatever powerful gods protect that scout guided the bullet into the heart of the leading warrior. You were the scout and Nah-kee-tats-an, my son, was the warrior you killed."

My jaw hangs open in horror. My lucky shot. The man I killed was my friend, Nah-kee-tats-an. Vivid pictures of the tall man leaped into my mind. I saw him in the moonlight by the river where we first met, at my campfire where he told me a story about my father, and at Casas Grandes where we fought side by side against the scalp hunters. "No!" I shout as if my denial can change the past.

"Yes," Wellington says quietly. "I told you once that our stories were intertwined, but my dreams did not tell me how. It is always hard to lose a son, but for an old man such as I who is nearing the end of his life, it is particularly difficult. My story is almost done and without Nah-kee-tats-an, there is no one to continue it. That is why I take you as a son, to continue my story as yours."

"But I'm not an Apache," I protest. "I come from a very different land, with its own stories."

"The stories of lands stay with the land. Land cannot move. Men may move and they take their stories with them. Your story and mine *are* different. We are different men from different worlds, but we are men. The gods have decreed that our stories be intertwined like braids of hair. There is nothing we can do to change that. Other braids—Nah-kee-tats-an's, Perdido's, your officer friend's—have been cut, but from this moment on, our braids, yours and mine, are one and will remain so until one of us is no more."

I struggle to understand what all of this means. "What happened?" I ask helplessly.

"Ghost Moon and I came to the river to see if the crossing was safe. We watched the soldiers hide and were about to leave when I saw you and the officer come forward."

"Where were you? We never saw anyone."

Ghost Moon laughs unpleasantly. "Just because you cannot see anyone does not mean that they cannot see you. It does not take much, even in open ground, to hide a man, especially if no one is looking for him."

"I recognized you," Wellington continued. "I said to Ghost Moon that we must capture you because you are my son. He scoffed. He wanted you dead. I told him no. We crawled up to where you lay on the hilltop and hid."

"How?" I ask. "We didn't see you."

Ghost Moon laughs again, but before he can say anything, Wellington goes on. "That is the trouble with you Americanos. You only look for one thing, so that is all you see. You are blind to everything else. You and the officer were expecting only a party of warriors to appear on the far horizon. Ghost Moon and I could have walked upright toward you and you would still not have seen us.

"We waited until you saw what you wanted, the warriors in the distance. Then Ghost Moon shot the officer and I hit you on the head."

"You hit me?"

"Of course. Would you have come if I had asked you?"

"No."

"Well, I hit you, not hard enough to break your skull, only so hard that you would sleep while we moved up the river and crossed where there were no soldiers. Now we are in Mexico and safe."

"I'm not safe," I say with sudden anger. "I've been kidnapped, and he wants to kill me." I point to Ghost Moon who smiles evilly back.

"You are safe, Busca. There will be no fighting with the army this side of the river, and you are safe from Ghost Moon. If he harms my son, he will gather much bad luck."

I look at Ghost Moon, wondering if bad luck is enough of an incentive for him not to kill me first chance he gets. It seems to be for now because, grumbling to himself, he gets up and goes over to join some other warriors roasting pieces of deer meat over a small fire. "What now?" I ask.

"We are tired and hungry. Your army would not let us rest. We have broken into many small parties. We will meet up and go deep into the mountains and rest. Then we will decide. Geronimo sits at San Carlos with the women and children. We are alone."

"And I will be your prisoner."

"You are not a prisoner, Busca."

"I'm tied up."

"There are many here who do not trust you. Like Ghost Moon, they think you should have died with the officer. They would not be pleased if you were not tied up this close to the river. When we get to the mountains you will be untied."

"And if I escape?"

"Where will you go? Besides, you will not escape. As I said, our stories are braided by the gods. You do not control your destiny. Now, I will get you some meat."

Wellington stands and walks over to the nearest fire. He moves remarkably easily for a man his age. Whatever Wellington means by his talk of our stories being intertwined, there's nothing I can do about it now. My head hurts, I'm securely tied up and I'm surrounded by people who would rather see me dead.

The thought of death conjures up an image of Lieutenant Fowler lying bleeding with Ghost Moon's arrow through his neck. Another of my friends dead. Two! Nah-kee-tats-an is dead as well, and I killed him. If the gods are controlling my destiny, why do they have to make it so cruel and why must I always be surrounded by death?

An aching loneliness creeps over me, not only because of my dead friends, but also because I find myself missing the Buffalo Soldiers. For many months, I have been a part of something, of a tight group of men who have shared all sorts of hardship, from grueling marches through brutal mountains to watching comrades killed and wounded by enemies who appear and disappear like ghosts. I had belonged.

Sergeant Rawlins's men would kill and die for each other without a second thought, and I had been one of them. Even if a trooper was killed, the survivors drew together to spread the loss among them all. His equipment was shared among his friends so that he would live on in their memory. Now I am alone with no one to kill or die for and every friend I have ever lost hanging unbearably heavy on me.

The only surviving friend I have is Wellington, my new father, and I have no idea what complex tragedy he is leading me into. Even his return with a sizzling hunk of succulent deer meat can't lift my black mood, and I chew morosely as I look at my bleak future.

# Tres Castillos, Mexico

**12 August, 1880**

The three rocky hills, one large and two small, rise like ruined castles from the grassy plain. Wickiups are scattered around the shore of a small lake that glistens blue in the afternoon sun. It's an idyllic scene, but I have been uncomfortable ever since we arrived here.

Of course, I hate being a prisoner, but it's not a harsh captivity. I'm not tied up anymore and can wander freely around the camp. That doesn't mean I am free though. There are dozens of miles of desert between me and anywhere I could escape to, and I'm surrounded by three hundred guards.

Ever since we arrived here, I have felt restless. Sudden noises, even the cries of the children, startle me. I continually catch myself scanning the far horizon without knowing what I am looking for, and the rocky hills scare me. I tell myself it's because of snakes, but that's a lie. Every time I approach one of the hills, particularly the largest one, a heavy, dark sense of dread settles on me, weighing me down, slowing my footsteps and, finally, forcing me back to the open lakeshore. And then there are the dreams.

Last night I dreamed I was alone, standing outside a vast castle. It was a European castle, the high walls cluttered with turrets, battlements and towers, like the pictures I had seen in the books I read as a kid about King Arthur and the Knights of the Round Table. I feel happy and walk across the drawbridge into the castle courtyard.

As soon as I am inside the walls, I am surrounded by terrifying, deafening noise—roaring, booming, thunderous noise. To my horror the castle begins to collapse around me. Huge blocks of stone crash to the ground, walls crumple into heaps of rubble and choking dust envelopes me. Frantically, I run in whatever direction seems safest, but there is no escape. Miraculously, although huge blocks of stone thud into the ground all around me, I am not hurt.

After what feels like an eternity, the dust clears. The castle is gone, and I am standing among the jumbled rocks on the large hill beside the camp. There is no one in sight, yet I have the strongest feeling that I am not alone.

As I look around, I hear a child's cry coming from behind a large rock to my left. The cry is like nothing I had ever heard before. The pity of it makes tears spring to my eyes, and I step forward to try and offer help. My foot slips and I grab a nearby rock to steady myself. I look down and see that the ground is a river of blood. All around me the very rocks are bleeding, and the child's wailing has become a cacophony of voices assaulting me from every direction. The voices cry, moan and plead for help, but I can do nothing. The river of blood rises over my ankles, to my knees and then my waist. The sounds increase until my ears ache. I know I am going to die and there is nothing I can do about it.

When I wake up after the dream, I am soaked in sweat and my cheeks are wet from tears. I stumble out of the wickiup I share with Wellington and stand in the predawn light, breathing heavily. In front of me the first rays of sunlight are painting the tops of the far mountains golden. Closer, the largest rocky hill stands, still in shadow, like some vengeful beast awaiting its chance to attack.

I have no idea what the dream means, if anything, but I can't wait to leave this place.

The leaders of the three hundred people camped here—Victorio, Lozen and Nana, an ancient warrior who has fought for more years than most others have been alive—sit in a circle with Wellington, myself, Ghost Moon and several others beside the lake.

The discussion has been lively and fast-paced but in Apache. I have learned a few words and Wellington whispers main points to me, but I have not understood much. Victorio has been mostly silent, listening intently as Lozen, Nana, Ghost Moon and the others talked. I'm wondering why Wellington brought me here, when Victorio suddenly addresses me in English. "What does Busca think on these matters?" he asks.

I'm so surprised that my mind goes blank, so Victorio continues. "Lozen says we should go toward the setting sun to the Sierra de la Candelaria. She says they are better to live in and closer to our homes at Warm Springs and Tularosa.

"Nana favors traveling toward the rising sun and the Sierra Madre, where Geronimo's cousin Juh lives with his band."

"Why are we asking this Americano?" Ghost Moon bursts out. He spits out *Americano* like poison. "We should kill him and go east. If Geronimo joins Juh, we will have enough warriors to defeat anyone the Americanos or Mexicans can send against us."

"You forget that Busca is Too-ah-yay-say's son," Lozen says. She has a strong voice, louder than her brother's, but she never shouts like Ghost Moon. She is a commanding presence when she speaks and can force the most aggressive opponent into silence with her piercing black eyes. Wellington has told me that, in addition to fighting as well as any man, she has the gift of sensing where enemies are and, several times, has given warnings to Victorio of impending attacks and ambushes before anyone has spotted the enemy.

"You also forget," she goes on, "that, even with Geronimo, and there is no guarantee that he will bring his people from San Carlos, we will be a mere two hundred and fifty warriors at most. That is but a drop in the river to the Americanos and Mexicans, and with all the women and children, we will need much food and we will not be able to move fast. We will win a few victories, but sooner or later they will catch us and no one will escape."

"The Sierra Madre Mountains are large," Nana says. According to Wellington, Nana is around eighty years old, and he looks it. His broad face is darkly weather-beaten and lined with wrinkles as deep as canyons, although his eyes still sparkle with life. His manner is calm and gentle, and he spends hours telling the children stories of their history. He is immensely respected, partly for his age and experience and partly because he has fought Americans and Mexicans for decades, beginning with the wars of Mangas Coloradas and Cochise.

"In their vastness," Nana continues, "we can spread ourselves out so that every small group can evade the Mexicans. We can wait for our brothers and be united in a common cause."

"A cause which is doomed to failure," Lozen says. "And we will be far from our homes and our land. If we go west, the Sierra de la Candelaria are also large, but there is more water and more game in them. We would be able to hunt more and raid less, so that the Mexicans would come after us less often."

"So we can wither peacefully," Ghost Moon interrupts scornfully. "We must keep raiding, to take back what is ours, and killing the Americanos and Mexicans who have invaded our land."

"Ghost Moon is rich in hatred," Wellington says. "This makes him a great warrior, but it blinds him. Since the first men with horses and swords came to our land, we have been fighting. We have killed countless of them, and they have killed the same of us. Yet they are still here, and those of us left are running from one mountain to another like rabbits chased by a coyote."

"I will go where it is decided," Ghost Moon says grudgingly, "but do not let the Americano say where we go. He is with us now because he has nowhere else to go and because he knows I would hunt him down and kill him slowly if he runs. But, Too-ah-yay-say's son or not, he will betray us at the first opportunity."

"Busca will not make any decisions," Victorio says in his soft voice, "but I would hear what he has to say. He is an Americano and does not think like us."

All eyes turn on me. I feel intensely uncomfortable. I take a deep breath and try to sound intelligent. "I *am* an Americano," I say, not thinking it worth drawing the distinction between Americanos and Canadians. "I cannot say what will be done on one day in one place, but I can say what the Buffalo Soldiers will do generally.

"Lozen is right. You may win a few victories, but the soldiers will not give up, and however many you kill, there will always be more. Look at the battle against Custer that you call the Greasy Grass. It was a great victory for the Sioux and Cheyenne, but it took two thousand warriors to defeat the few hundred troopers with Custer. You can never get that many warriors together, even with Geronimo."

"The Americanos and Mexicans cannot get as many soldiers as Custer did," Ghost Moon interrupts.

"That is true," I say calmly, "but look at what happened after the Greasy Grass. Less than two years later, Crazy Horse was dead and Sitting Bull and Gall fled to Canada. The sacred lands had been given to miners and the people crammed onto reservations." I'm trying to remember bits and pieces I read in newspapers and I'm not sure I've got all the details right, but what I say is making an impact. I see Victorio and Lozen nodding.

"Even a great victory like the Greasy Grass," I continue, "much bigger than you can hope for wherever you go, did not stop the Sioux and Cheyenne being forced onto reservations away from their sacred land."

"So you suggest that we return to San Carlos like whipped dogs with our tails between our legs?" Ghost Moon asks with a sneer.

"No," I reply. "It is not for me to suggest what you should do. I am simply saying that I think that the Americanos and Mexicans will not give up and that you cannot win everything that you wish for."

"I have listened to all the talk," Victorio says. "It is not easy to say what is the right thing to do, but we will head for the Sierra de la Candelaria. We need to recover our strength and the hunting is better there. We shall also be closer to Warm Springs and the Chiricahua lands if"—he emphasizes the *if* and looks hard at Ghost Moon—"if we decide then that we must return there."

Victorio stands and the meeting is over.

"You spoke well, Busca." I turn to see Wellington standing nearby.

"I hope so," I say, "but I don't know what will happen."

"No one but the gods do. We do what we can."

"Why did you make me your son?"

"It was what I was meant to do," Wellington replies enigmatically.

"But why am I here? What am I supposed to do?" The memory of last night's dream is weighing heavily on me.

"Whatever you do will be what the gods wish."

"I'm sick of the gods," I growl, standing up. "They're an excuse for anything, and I don't want them controlling my life."

"You have no choice."

Wellington's calm simply makes me angrier. "I do have choices. I'm not Perdido, a corpse sitting in a cave while you tell your stupid stories. I'm free. I can make my own choices." I'm deliberately trying to annoy Wellington and make him angry. It doesn't work.

"Sons often fight with fathers," he says with an infuriating smile. "One day you will see what your road is to be."

Wellington turns and walks away, leaving me helplessly fuming while, all around, people are preparing for travel. I stay where I am, staring at the rocky hill looming over us. At least we'll be leaving here, but I can't help wondering if I've said the right thing and who will die as a result of my advice.

# Sierra de la Candelaria Mountains, Mexico

**15 September, 1880**

The first volley of rifle fire drops the two leading warriors before anyone can react. The rest of us slide from our mounts and spread out into the rocks on either side of the trail. The boys lead the horses away out of danger. I estimate from the rate of fire that there are no more than five or six men shooting, but they are well hidden in the rocks higher up the valley, and I can see nothing.

Victorio is everywhere, running from rock to rock giving instructions. Half a dozen warriors move off to either side and begin scaling the canyon walls, hoping to outflank our attackers. The eight of us remaining keep low. Ghost Moon and several others take turns jumping up onto rocks and screaming taunts at the enemy, holding their attention while the flankers work their way up the canyon. We do not fire back; ammunition is too valuable.

I sit behind my rock and feel miserable. It has been a grueling journey here from Tres Castillos. In the first few days we were discovered and had to split the party into several smaller groups. Ever since then, it has been a continual cat-and-mouse game, dodging squads of Mexican cavalry and parties of local ranchers eager to trap us and sell our scalps in Chihuahua. Because of Victorio's, Lozen's and Nana's skill, they haven't trapped us, but it has cost us all our supplies, ammunition and many horses.

We had hoped that things would be easier when we reached the mountains, but it doesn't seem so. Victorio has led our party on ahead to the spring in this canyon, but it seems we were expected and it is guarded. If we cannot get water here, things will be serious. The women and children are waiting in a canyon nearby, and they and the horses are as desperate as we were when I came south with Morrow before we reached the Corralitos River.

I laugh quietly to myself. That time I was a scout for the 10th US Cavalry. Now I'm thinking like an Apache. It would be fairly easy for me to sneak away through the rough ground and try to join the Mexicans firing on us, but I don't. First, I'm dressed like an Apache warrior and would probably be shot before I could explain.

Second, I'm not certain I want to. In the last few weeks I have suffered alongside these people around me and I feel a kinship with them. Wellington is even teaching me more of the language. We have been through the same hardships while the men farther up the canyon have tried to kill us. A bond has formed, similar to the one I felt with Sergeant Rawlins and the Buffalo Soldiers. It is a thing that is not easily broken.

Perhaps if I had a family and a stable life somewhere else, that would foster a stronger desire to escape, but I don't. These people in this canyon are the only family I have. I even feel a grudging respect for Ghost Moon as he leaps onto rocks and challenges the Mexicans to shoot him.

So far, in what skirmishes there have been, I have managed not to fight. I am allowed my Colt revolver but haven't fired it. What will I do when these skirmishes become full-scale battles? Will I shoot Mexican soldiers to protect Wellington? If it comes to it, will I shoot my own countrymen, the Buffalo Soldiers? I don't know. I just pray it never comes to that.

A short, intense burst of firing from up the canyon interrupts my thoughts. It is followed by some screams, and then a warrior appears on a rock, waving his rifle. All around me figures rise from hiding and begin moving up the canyon.

The spring that the Mexican soldiers were guarding is little more than a trickle at the base of a muddy bank, but the warriors drink greedily from the pool that has formed below it. After we are satisfied, several men begin the laborious task of filling the assortment of containers we have brought. They range from wine-skins to battered US Army canteens.

I wander off through the rocks. The bodies of four Mexican soldiers lie crumpled behind rocks. They have been stripped of anything of value—weapons, ammunition, jackets, trousers, boots. They have all been shot, but two show stab wounds as well and one has an arrow embedded in his chest. Splashes of blood stain the rocks.

I'm feeling miserable. It's one thing to think about possibly having to shoot one person to save another, but the sight of the bodies—men who, under slightly different circumstances, I might have had to kill today to protect my friends—brings home what killing means. It's not a simple, clean event, but a complex, messy tragedy that doesn't go away.

I wander farther away, bleakly remembering the men I have killed: the Kid outside Tucson, Roberto Ramirez and the others at Casas Grandes, Nah-kee-tats-an. All were either self-defence or accidental, but that doesn't make me feel any easier. Their faces still float accusingly before me when I lie awake and miserable in the blackness before dawn.

I'm distracted by a whimper from higher up the canyon wall. Scrambling over the rocks, I track it down to a wounded Mexican soldier. His scalp on the left side has been torn open by a bullet and he is covered in blood, but he's still alive and watches me with wide, frightened eyes. A rifle is lying on the ground beside him but out of reach.

The soldier is young, if anything, even younger than me. He is clutching a small silver crucifix to his chest. "*Sea tranquilo, joven*," I say, urging him to stay calm as I approach and kneel by him. "*Mi nombre es Jim*," I say.

"Jose," the boy whispers. I give him a drink from my canteen. He drinks gratefully. I'm wondering what else I can do to help him, when he lets go of his crucifix, reaches up and weakly grabs my shirt. "*Usted debe irse*," he says with great effort. "*Los soldados están cerca.*"

"You're telling me to leave? How near are the soldiers? *¿Qué tan cerca están los soldados?*"

The boy raises his right arm with great effort and points over the ridge behind us. "*Dos, tres kilómetros.*"

"*¿Cuántos?*"

"*Cien.*"

"A hundred," I say, standing up. These men are just an advance party. There are a hundred Mexican soldiers only a few kilometers away over the ridge. They must have heard the firing. How long will it take them to scale the ridge? I look around nervously. Everything's quiet.

"*Vaya*," the boy says.

"Yes," I say. "Thank you. *Gracias.*" I scramble back to the spring as fast as I can.

Victorio is standing, urging the men filling the canteens to hurry. I grab him by the arm. In an instant, Lozen is beside me, her knife at my throat.

"Soldiers," I gasp breathlessly. "Mexican soldiers, over the ridge maybe two or three kilometers away."

Victorio doesn't bother to ask me how I know but barks orders in Apache. Ghost Moon and two others head off toward the top of the ridge while the rest grab canteens and equipment and head down the canyon.

When we reach the valley where the boys are holding the horses, Victorio sends most of the men out to make contact with the main party. Five of us wait for Ghost Moon and his companions with their horses.

I am happy. I managed to warn my friends of danger and didn't have to kill anyone. The Mexican soldiers will find the boy and tend to his wounds. Perhaps not everything has to end badly.

Soon I see three figures loping toward us over the plain. Without breaking stride, Ghost Moon reaches us and vaults onto his pony. He lets out a long string of Apache while pointing back at the canyon.

"You were right," Victorio says, turning to me. "There were many Mexicans climbing the other side of the ridge. Fortunately, they could not bring their horses, so we have time to escape north. Thank you."

Victorio wheels his horse and heads off. The others follow. I smile to myself, glad at Victorio's thanks.

"Hey, Busca." I look around to see Ghost Moon riding past me. For a moment I think the smile on his scarred face is of thanks. Then he holds up the small silver crucifix dangling from a thin chain, laughs and rides after Victorio.

## 5 October, 1880

Some hundred and fifty of us stand, sit and lie in a wide, rough circle on the desert floor. To the east, heavy black thunderheads pile up along the edge of the mountains, which have not given the security we seek. Knifelike lightning and rolling thunder bear down on us as inexorably as the soldiers who have tormented and harried us over the past weeks.

We are exhausted and starvation haunts us like a wolf snapping at our heels. Our clothing is in rags, and the children's eyes stare with hunger. The hunting has been poor. We have very little ammunition left, but it doesn't matter—we can't risk firing rifles at any game we see for fear of attracting the soldiers who hunt us.

Our few remaining horses stand in a forlorn group to one side, ribs sticking out and heads hanging desolately. I notice a young woman who gave birth just yesterday. Her husband was killed in a skirmish weeks ago and she is hugging the tiny wrapped bundle to her chest. Her eyes dart around nervously.

Several groups have split off to try and work their way north, back onto the reservation where, at least, the children will be fed. Victorio and Nana have managed to keep the rest together, but a decision must be made:

go north back to the reservation or east to find Juh in the Sierra Madre.

In the center of the circle, Lozen stands, arms spread wide and head thrown back. She is dressed as a warrior, in patched breeches and grubby shirt, and her long black hair hangs lank and dirty down her back. Like all of us, her face is thinner, but in her case it makes her look more powerful, enhancing her high cheekbones and dark, deep-set eyes. Slowly, she begins stamping her bare feet, throwing up tiny storms of dust. Gradually the others also begin stamping until there is a regular pounding beat and the air is filled with dust.

Without altering the rhythm of her feet, Lozen begins to turn. As she does so, she chants her prayer to the god Ussen. I have learned enough words from Wellington to understand roughly what it means.

*Upon this earth*
*On which we live*
*Ussen has Power*
*This Power is mine*
*For locating the enemy.*
*I search for that Enemy*
*Which only Ussen the Great*
*Can show to me.*

As she chants, the heavy clouds roll over us, darkening the sky until it is as if night has fallen in the middle of the afternoon. After three rotations, Lozen stands facing south. Her arms begin to quiver until her hands shake visibly. A murmur runs through the watchers. Lozen rotates ninety degrees to face west, into the heart of the thunderstorm. The quivering begins once more. She repeats the movement, facing north. Once more the quivering. Only when she faces east do Lozen's hands remain still.

For an age, Lozen stands like a statue while everyone else keeps the thumping beat with their feet. A stark flash of lightning and an almost simultaneous crash of thunder seem to wake her up. I can smell the sharp metallic tang of the storm and feel the first large drops of rain. Lozen drops her arms and the crowd falls silent.

Lozen begins speaking as she slowly rotates, staring all the while at the people. "Ussen has shown me our enemies. They are few to the west in the mountains but many to the north and south. They plan to catch us in a trap."

"Sister." Victorio steps forward. "There are none to the east?"

Lozen shakes her head. The rain is heavier now, large drops splashing on the ground around her.

Victorio sighs. "Then we shall head east. There are ranches and towns we can raid for supplies. We will return to Tres Castillos and rest there. Then we will find Juh and see if Geronimo will join us."

A murmur of agreement runs around the circle. It will be a hard journey, but the hope of escaping the soldiers and joining the rest of the people is strong.

The rain is torrential now. The lightning is blinding against the dark clouds and the ground trembles from the thunder.

"I will not go with you," Lozen says. Everyone falls silent and stares at her. This is serious. Lozen is our eyes and ears. Countless times, her gift of being able to divine where and how many of our enemies are nearby has enabled us to escape capture. She walks over to the woman with the newborn infant. "This child will die in the desert," she proclaims. "I will take the child and the mother north to the reservation. I will find you to the east."

"This is just one child," Ghost Moon speaks out. "For it you would abandon the rest of the band?"

"There are few of us left," Lozen says, meeting Ghost Moon's eyes, "and there will be fewer. Every child is of great consequence. This infant is our people, our future. Is that not worth more than our band?"

Lozen stares at Ghost Moon until he drops his eyes and turns away. Lozen addresses everyone. "You will not need me on the journey east. The soldiers will not expect you to return to Tres Castillos. You will have a good start, and in the open desert, a good pair of eyes can see as far as my gift. I will rejoin you. And I will talk with Geronimo and the others."

"What about the soldiers to the north?" I blurt out. Over the weeks we have been together, I have come to admire this strange, mystical woman. She exudes power and I will miss her as much as the others. I don't want her to be killed or, worse, captured by the soldiers who are hunting us.

Lozen fixes me with an unblinking stare. A lank strand of hair has fallen across her cheek, but she makes no attempt to brush it aside. Something about her expression makes me feel like a stupid child. I lower my eyes, wishing I had kept quiet.

Lozen's laugh rings out over the drumming of the raindrops. It is such an unusual sound—I have only ever heard her laugh in private when she is with her brother—that everyone stares. I look up.

"When first you joined us, Busca, I did not trust you. I thought that Ghost Moon was right in wishing you dead, but Too-ah-yay-say and my brother spoke for you. You are not one of us. You never will be. But you have not been an enemy and you try to learn our ways and our language. As long as my people fight your people, there is a chance that I may have to kill you, but for now you are my friend.

"I am Lozen, my brother's right hand. As long as there are soldiers, I will have a horse. As long as there are ranches with cattle and I have my knife, I will have meat. As long as there are clouds in the sky, I will have water. Do not worry about me."

I notice that Victorio and several others round about are smiling at me. I feel a fool, but also oddly honored that Lozen has called me her friend.

"We will leave here as soon as the storm passes," Victorio says to the crowd. "For now lay out whatever you have to collect the water that the gods are giving us." He and Lozen move off to one side and talk urgently as people busy themselves getting ready for the journey. By the time the storm ends, Lozen and the woman with the newborn baby are walking north and our bedraggled party is straggling east.

I'm glad to be leaving the mountains behind as it has been a hard time these past weeks, yet the mention of returning to Tres Castillos unsettles me. I try to shrug it off, but my dreams of collapsing castles and death nag at the back of my mind.

# Casas Grandes, Mexico

11 October, 1880

"I have always wished to come here," Wellington says. We are sitting in the ruins of what must once have been an impressive three- or four-story structure. The main group is traveling to the south, farther from the modern town, but Wellington wanted to come here and he asked me to accompany him.

"The ancients lived here long before there were Apaches or Spaniards or Mexicans or Americans. They built cities of wonder." Wellington waves his arm to encompass the impressive walls that surround us. "Yet, where are they now?"

I shrug helplessly and Wellington continues. "There was a world before the gods made people, and there will be a world after we are all gone. It is good to remember that."

Wellington sits in silent contemplation, and my mind begins to wander. It's a strange feeling for me, returning so close to the ruined hacienda where the story of my father reached its bloody conclusion. I am tempted to visit the hacienda, but there are too many memories there, both of Roberto Ramirez and my friend Nah-kee-tats-an. Besides, it would be too dangerous—I look more like an Apache warrior now than a cowboy.

So much has happened since I was here nearly three years ago. I find it difficult to believe I was ever so innocent. Since then I have seen the depths to which men, of all cultures, can sink and, less commonly, the heights to which they can rise. I know how complicated the world can be. How could I not after all that has happened to me? I laugh out loud.

"Laughter is good, Busca," Wellington says with a smile, "but what do you find amusing in this place?"

"I was wondering what my mother and the good people I grew up with in Yale would think if they could see me now, dressed like an Apache warrior and being hunted and chased by the army."

"They would be surprised. Do you wish to go home?"

"Home?" The question takes me by surprise. "I don't have a home. Certainly nothing as solid as the houses the ancients built. My father's dead, and my mother has sold the house I grew up in and married the local storekeeper. Everywhere I have been since I left Yale is too loaded with memories."

"Then you must become like a turtle, Busca. You must carry your home upon your back."

"I suppose," I say, amused by the idea. "Today I share this home with the ghosts of the ancients. Tomorrow my home will be on Coronado's back. The day after Tres Castillos. I suppose it means I will never own very much."

"It also means that you will never have much that people can take away from you. It is as I told you when we first met. Your stories are your most treasured possession; no one can ever take them from you.

"I will tell you a story, Busca. Once, when the world was very young, the Creator and White Painted Woman had a child. White Painted Woman called him Child of Water. When Child of Water was a baby, his mother had to hide him because there were four monsters in the world at that time who would eat him if they found him. There was a Giant, a Bull, an Eagle and Prairie Dogs, and they surrounded Child of Water to the north, south, east and west. But Child of Water was very clever, and he fought each of the monsters in turn and defeated and killed them all."

Wellington falls silent, and I wait patiently for him to continue. "When I was little, my mother told me the stories of how Child of Water defeated and killed the four monsters. She told me that, because of this, there were no more monsters in the world to scare me, but she was wrong. There are no more Giants or Bulls or Eagles or Prairie Dogs that eat people, but there are still monsters.

"I think, when Child of Water killed the four monsters, they broke apart and the pieces all went into the hearts of people. Some people received small pieces and others large, but everybody got some. We are the monsters now, but there is no Child of Water to help us."

Wellington turns his gaze full on me. "You and I are like Child of Water now, surrounded by monsters in all directions. These monsters are strong, and I do not think we will escape them."

"We've escaped them before," I say, worried about Wellington's pessimism and wondering where he is going with his story.

"Nana's scouts say there are Mexicans to our west and south, but to our north there are Buffalo Soldiers who have once more crossed the Rio Grande River. They are not far away, perhaps only a day's ride."

Wellington stands up and stretches his stiff limbs. He looks up at the sky through the ruined walls of the building. "I must go and tend to my horse."

I'm confused by the sudden change in topic, but Wellington continues before I can think of something to say. "I am old and slow. If a young man were to take his horse and ride away to the north, there is nothing I could do to stop him."

Wellington walks out a break in the wall, leaving me to ponder what he has said. He's offering me a chance to escape, to head north and find the Buffalo Soldiers. Perhaps Sergeant Rawlins and the others I rode and fought beside are there, a few hours hard riding away. This is the first good chance I have had to escape since I was captured beside the Rio Grande. I should take it. Shouldn't I?

North or south? To the north are the Buffalo Soldiers I scouted for. I miss them and I would be welcomed if I rejoined them. They would take me back to New Mexico Territory with them. There I would be with my own people and would have choices. I could stay as a scout or leave the army and find work. I could travel back up to Canada or anywhere else the fancy took me.

To the south is Victorio's band where I will always be an outsider, even though I have shared many hardships with them. With Victorio I have no choices; I must lead the life of a fugitive, harried this way and that by enemy soldiers until everyone is either killed or captured and sent back to the reservation. Heading north is the sensible thing to do.

I stand and go outside. Wellington is busy with his horse, deliberately not looking at me. I tend to Coronado and mount. Wellington looks up. "Be quick," I say to him. "It's a long way to catch up to Victorio before nightfall."

Wellington's wrinkled face breaks into a smile and he nods. He climbs into his saddle and we set off to the south.

"I knew you would make this decision, Busca," Wellington says as we ride out of Casas Grandes. "There was no other way for you to go."

"Perhaps," I say, not comfortable with the idea that I have no part in the decisions I make. "But you are right about stories—once we are in one, we need to see it through to the end. How do your dreams tell you this story will end?"

Wellington is silent for a long time as we trot out into the desert. "It troubles me that my dreams do not show me the ending of this story. Maybe the gods think it is too sad for us to bear before it happens."

"You told me once that you had dreamed the end of your story," I say.

"My story ends in death, as do all stories," Wellington says with a regretful smile. "What I cannot see is the fate of those around me."

"I have been having dreams. They began when we were last at Tres Castillos; then they went away, but they began once more last night." I tell Wellington about the dream I had about the collapsing castle and the rocks bleeding. "What does it mean?"

"It takes a great sadness for rocks to bleed," Wellington says. I try to get him to say more but he refuses, and we ride in silence for the rest of the day. I had hoped that Wellington could explain away my dream, but instead it seems to have bothered him instead. I regret mentioning it. Perhaps dreams should be kept secret.

Talking about my dream has left me with a horrible sense of foreboding and the idea that I have made a dreadful mistake in not running away to the Buffalo Soldiers. However, my decision is made. I must see the story out, whatever the consequences.

# Near Tres Castillos, Mexico

13 October, 1880

**N**o!" I hurl myself at Ghost Moon, grabbing the arm that holds the club. We crash to the ground and roll. The young Mexican boy breaks free and runs. I have both my hands wrapped around Ghost Moon's wrist and I'm hanging on for dear life. If he gets his arm free, the club will crush my skull in seconds.

We roll around, Ghost Moon kicking and gouging at me and me hanging on until an imperious voice breaks in. "Is this what we have come to?" Victorio asks. "Do we now, surrounded by enemies, fight amongst ourselves? Cease!"

I feel Ghost Moon relax. I let go, roll away and jump to my feet. Ghost Moon rises more slowly and stands, staring at me with undisguised hatred.

Wellington stands to one side, clutching the terrified boy's arm. Behind him, the boy's parents lie dead on the ground in front of their hacienda, and several Apache warriors are busy rounding up horses and cattle in the corral.

"What goes on here?" Victorio asks.

"Ghost Moon was going to kill the boy," I blurt out.

Victorio looks long and hard at me. "That is his right. We came here for horses and cattle. The boy is an enemy."

"The soldiers who hunt us are enemies," I say. "Perhaps even the boy's parents who ranch on this land, but the boy is no more than six or seven years old. He is nobody's enemy."

"He will grow up to be a man and to kill Apaches," Ghost Moon snarls at me.

"What honor is there in killing him?" I ask. Ghost Moon takes a threatening step toward me. "That makes you no better than the scalp hunters who slaughtered children and sold their scalps as those of warriors."

Ghost Moon is having considerable difficulty stopping himself from leaping at me with his club. Only Victorio's presence is preventing him. Several warriors have come over to see what the commotion's about and form a loose circle around us.

"What would you have us do, Busca?" Victorio asks.

"Spare the boy's life."

Victorio nods. "And what will you pay for this boy's life?"

"Pay?" I ask in confusion.

"Would you pay your life for his?"

"I...I don't know," I stammer.

"Then you must decide, Busca. Ghost Moon wishes to kill the child, and you wish to spare him. Are you prepared to fight to save him?"

An evil smile forms on Ghost Moon's scarred face and he visibly relaxes. Me being Wellington's son cannot prevent this. This is his chance to revenge himself for the burn I gave him.

I'm confused and scared. I hadn't thought but simply reacted to save the boy. Now, suddenly I am faced with a hideous, terrifying decision: fight a man who is stronger and more skillful than me, and who wants little more than to see me dead, or stand by and watch a child killed.

I look from Ghost Moon's predatory smile to the boy's tear-stained, frightened face. The boy is staring wide-eyed at me. He's just seen his parents killed and come within an inch of death himself. There's no decision to make. I look over at Wellington. His face is impassive. He doesn't know how this story will end.

"I'll fight," I say, and Ghost Moon's smile widens.

"Choose a weapon, Busca," Victorio says. Ghost Moon hefts his club comfortably in his hand. It's made of wood. The handle is over a foot long and the head is a polished knot of hard wood, larger than my fist. A tassel of black horsehair streams from the base of the handle. I have no weapon except my revolver, and I can't use that. I look around helplessly. The gathered warriors stare back impassively. It's not their concern. If I have no weapon it will simply be easier for Ghost Moon to kill me.

The boy suddenly twists away from Wellington's grip and darts over to his father's body. He hesitates at the corpse but then crouches and pulls a long knife from his belt. He scuttles back over and hands the knife to me.

It's a hunting knife, the blade curved for slicing the skin off an antelope, but the blade is heavy too—heavy enough to crack deer bones—and it has a sharp point for working into a carcass's joints. It's a working knife not a fighting knife, but that'll make no difference. I've never been in any kind of knife fight.

"*Gracias*," I say to the boy. He smiles shyly and backs away.

I watch him go, and that almost costs me my life. Ghost Moon lunges forward, swinging the club at my head. I only just manage to duck in time, but I'm off balance. The return swing is fast and catches me a painful blow on my left shoulder, sending arrows of pain down my arm.

I drop to the ground and roll, slashing at where I think Ghost Moon's legs are, but he's gone and the knife sweeps through empty air. I keep rolling and jump to my feet in crouch and skip to one side. I feel the wind from the club as it passes my ear. I drop and roll in the opposite direction and sweep with the knife. I'm rewarded by a yelp of pain and see a bright splash of blood on Ghost Moon's arm. It doesn't slow him. His leg arcs up and his foot catches me painfully in the ribs. I manage to keep my balance and dance two steps away from the swinging club.

We stand a couple of paces apart, breathing heavily and staring at each other. There is a tear in Ghost Moon's shirt and a patch of blood on his upper arm where I caught him, but it's minor. On the other hand, my ribs hurt with every deep breath I take, and my left arm is numb and almost useless.

We circle warily, each making minor feints to keep our opponent off balance. Ghost Moon lunges at me. I react, but then he drops unexpectedly and swings his club at my leg. I jump, but the handle of the club catches my left ankle. Once more I drop and roll out of the way before coming to my feet.

Ghost Moon smiles at me. He's toying with me, weakening me until he's ready to finish me off. I'm only still alive because I've been fast and lucky, but I'm hurting and tiring. It won't be long. I have to do something.

I step to my left, hoping to draw my opponent that way before I change direction and lunge at him with the knife, but my injured ankle gives way and I collapse to my knees. Luckily I see the club coming and duck, but I know Ghost Moon's tactics now— the club will sweep back immediately and lower. I slash the heavy knife blade up with all my strength to where I think the blow will come. The blade isn't even directed the right way for cutting, but its weight hits something and there's a dull crack. I hear Ghost Moon gasp and the club lands heavily on the ground beside me.

Painfully, I haul myself to my feet and kick the club away. Ghost Moon stands, hunched over, clutching his right forearm to his stomach. His wrist is bent at an unnatural angle. In obvious pain, my enemy stands up straight and stares me in the eye.

"You may kill him, Busca," Victorio says.

"No," I say tiredly. "There are too few warriors left. We fought and I won. The boy will live?"

"The boy will live," Victorio confirms.

I look at Ghost Moon. He nods.

It takes all my remaining strength not to collapse, but I turn, drop the knife and limp away. The circle of warriors parts to let me through.

I hear footsteps and the boy tugs at my sleeve. I look down and he hands me his father's knife. I take it and keep going, without even the strength to feel glad that I have won and am still alive. Tomorrow we will be at Tres Castillos and my dreams.

# Tres Castillos, Mexico

**Afternoon, 14 October, 1880**

The scene in front of me looks tranquil. A large fire is burning and several warriors are busy butchering one of the cows we took from the *ranchería* yesterday. Wickiups are being hastily built, and a laughing group of women and children are bathing and splashing in the small lake. This is the first time we've been able to relax in weeks, and Victorio has said we will stay here for three days before moving on to the Sierra Madre. He says it is so we can rest, and we *do* need that, but I wonder if he's hoping that Lozen will rejoin us.

I sit with my back against a rock at the base of the largest of the three hills, the Mexican boy beside me. The feeling has returned to my left arm, but there is a large, livid bruise on my shoulder where Ghost Moon's club caught me; my ribs still ache from his kick; and my ankle is swollen. But none of this bothers me. I'm simply happy to be alive.

Wellington says the boy is mine now since I saved his life, and I joked that that makes him Wellington's grandson. I'm glad I saved the boy's life, but I hadn't planned on taking on the responsibility for him. I had assumed he would be left at the ranchería, but Victorio insisted we take him with us, and the boy showed no sign of wanting to be left. Since the fight, he hasn't spoken a word or strayed more than six feet away from me. I've told him he's safe, but he doesn't listen, trotting along beside me as I limp about and sitting gazing up at me when, as now, I sit still. I'm going to have to get him back to his own people, but I have no idea how.

I idly scan the camp. Nana and some twenty warriors are away on an extended hunting expedition. They took almost all our remaining ammunition and left from the ranchería we attacked yesterday, making as broad and obvious a trail as they could to draw anyone who was following us away from Tres Castillos. The rest of us, some sixty-five warriors and almost a hundred women and children, arrived here at noon. Victorio is confident that we have escaped the net, at least for the time being. I would feel more confident if Lozen were here with her powers of divining where our enemies are.

Across the lake, our horses and pack mules graze, happy to have food and water and not being ridden over the barren desert. I've just recently tended to Coronado, brushing him down as best I can and talking to him. He's skinny but has survived the hardships of our travel better than many of the mounts.

As the sun lowers toward dusk in the western sky, I try to retain the feeling of contentment and push back memories of the dark dreams that plagued my mind when we last camped here. I can't rid myself of the feeling that, however safe we may be here, this story is drawing to a close.

"And how is my family," Wellington says with a grin as he perches himself on a rock beside us.

"Well," I say, although the boy huddles closer in against me. He does this whenever an Apache comes near, even Wellington. "Are we safe here?"

"Only Lozen could tell us that."

"What do your dreams tell you?"

"My dreams tell only of me, but I have seen myself with Nana, Juh and Geronimo in the Sierra Madre."

"So Geronimo *will* join us there?"

Wellington shrugs. "What will you do with your son?" He nods at the boy.

"He's not my son," I say, "but I will try and return him to his people."

"And will you go with him back to your people?" Wellington asks.

"I suppose, ultimately, I must." I've thought about this a lot since Wellington offered me my freedom at Casas Grandes. The same thing that stopped me leaving then is stopping me now: a feeling that the story isn't over and that there is still something I have to do. After the fight with Ghost Moon, I wondered if that something was saving the boy's life, but the feeling hasn't gone away. All I can do is wait.

The delicious smell of roasting beef wafts over me from the fire, making my mouth water. Wellington, apparently satisfied with my brief answer to his inquiry about what I will do, stands up and wanders off. The boy relaxes. I lean my head back against the rock and close my eyes. Whatever is going to happen, I will enjoy this cool evening with safety and plenty to eat and drink.

## Dusk, 14 October, 1880

I must have drifted off into sleep, because it's already dusk when the hellish crash of gunfire startles me awake. People are running in all directions in panic, splashing out of the lake, gathering children and grabbing whatever weapons are to hand. Already, several warriors are running to the edge of the camp and firing back at the, so far, invisible attackers. Victorio stands in the middle of the camp, directing warriors to the growing firing line and ordering the women and children to take shelter among the rocks of the largest hill. Already there are bodies scattered over the ground.

I grab the boy by the arm and drag him up in among the rocks of the hill. Everyone else is streaming toward the hill to find shelter from the flying bullets.

One group of warriors is working its way around the lake toward the horses. As I watch, a squad of Mexican cavalry breaks from behind a low hill and charges. They cut in front of our horses and drive the warriors back.

In barely more time than it takes to tell, the plain between the hill and the lake is empty apart from the still-blazing fire, the wickiups and half a dozen prone, lifeless bodies. For all its violence, the scene is remarkably quiet. I can hear people moving around the hill, clambering over rocks, and I can hear the firing, which is much less now and sounds far away. Beside me, the boy whimpers softly. In the distance, black against the darkening landscape, I can see mounted figures moving closer, scores of them.

"Come," I say to the boy, "we must climb to the top of the hill. *Subimos a la cima de la colina*," I repeat in Spanish when he doesn't move. He's so still that, for a moment, I think he's been hit by a stray bullet. Then he speaks. The first time since the ranchería.

"*¿Quiénes son esos hombres?*" he asks.

"Those men are soldiers. *Son soldados*," I reply.

"*¿Nos matarán?*" he asks.

"*¿Matarán?*" I ask.

The boy draws his finger across his throat. "*Muerto*," he says.

"No," I say, horrified at the question. "No, they won't kill us. *No nos matarán*." I try to sound as convincing as possible, but I'm far from certain. "Come." I take the boy's hand and lead him up between the rocks, where women and children hide and warriors peer out into the gathering dark. The boy follows without complaint.

At the top of the hill, there's a flat area surrounded by large rocks. Victorio, Wellington, Ghost Moon and several others are already there. Ghost Moon stares at me as I arrive. His right wrist is strapped in leather thongs, and he holds it across his chest. His club dangles from his left hand.

"They are all around," Ghost Moon says, turning back to Victorio. "Many hundreds, and they have our horses. We are trapped like rats. All they need do is wait until what little ammunition we have is gone and then they can come in and kill us at their leisure." Ghost Moon points his club at me. "And it is this man's fault. They have followed the boy he would not let me kill."

Is it true? Am I responsible for all these people being trapped here and for what will happen?

"No," Victorio's soft voice commands attention. "It is not Busca's fault. Our scouts saw no one follow us. They were waiting. They knew we would come here. Only Lozen could have warned us."

Victorio closes his eyes and bows his head as if a great weight has descended on him, the weight of responsibility for all the people here and what will happen to them. There's no escape this time. Victorio has failed. His war is over.

"What will happen?" I ask. "Will we be sent back to the reservation?"

Ghost Moon laughs unpleasantly. "You are a lucky fighter, but, like all Americanos, you are an innocent. Your Buffalo Soldiers would capture us and take us back to San Carlos. Those are Mexicans out there." He sweeps his club in a circle. "We have fought against them since before there were Americans in this land. They do not have reservations."

"At dawn they will come," Victorio adds, raising his head to look at me. "Every warrior will be killed and his scalp sold in the square at Chihuahua City. The women and children will be sold as slaves. Our deaths and servitude will make men rich."

"Are you glad now to be Too-ah-yay-say's son?" Ghost Moon asks. "Many times, Busca, since we met by the fire that night, I have wished you dead. Every time I have bent to drink water from a still pool, I have been reminded of my hatred for you. But that is nothing now. My scarred face, my arm, our fight, my hatred are but dust in a desert wind. The storm will come tomorrow and blow our dust into the next world. We shall sell our lives as dearly as possible, but it will be cheap without ammunition for our rifles. My regret is that I cannot draw a bow to take our attackers with us."

I shiver in the darkness. A bullet whines over our heads. On the plain I can see the flickering fires of our besiegers as they settle in for the night, resting before they collect their bounty in the morning. A huge full moon, silver pale and ghostly, sits on top of the distant hills, watching.

I step forward and pull my cavalry revolver from my belt. Ghost Moon tenses. I grip it by the barrel and offer it to my old enemy. "It has my last six bullets in it," I say. "Now you can fight."

Ghost Moon stares at the weapon for a long time. Eventually, he places his club on the ground and takes it. He looks up at me and smiles. I think it is the first time I have seen a genuine smile cross his twisted features. "Thank you, Busca," he says.

I nod and, with the boy at my side, move down the hill to find somewhere to spend the long night to come.

## Dawn, 15 October, 1880

"Did you sleep well, Busca?" Wellington is crouched beside me.

"No," I reply miserably. "How can anyone sleep on a night like this?"

Wellington nods at the boy curled up in the darkness beside me, fast asleep. "The innocent, Busca."

"Then I am not innocent," I say, carefully standing so as not to disturb the boy. I haven't slept a wink, lying in the darkness on the hard ground listening to the sounds of the people around me and the occasional distant rifle shots, and worrying what the sun will bring. I look over at the eastern horizon where a knife-edge of light is brightening above the hills. I won't have to wait long to find out.

"You said that nothing would happen here," I say accusingly. I'm feeling utterly miserable—angry at all the mistakes I've made, grief-stricken at all the friends I've lost and guilty at my role in so many deaths. I'm also scared of what is about to happen, and I try and take it out on Wellington.

"You misunderstood me, Busca. My dreams showed me only what happens to me. I saw no one else in them. But I fear many stories will end this day."

The boy stirs and looks around sleepily. He stretches and stands beside me. I make a silent promise to myself that, whatever happens to me, I will make certain that the boy survives this day.

It's light enough now to make out movement on the plain around our refuge. Dark figures are gathering over where the soldiers camped. There's no sense of urgency. They want it to be fully light by the time they enter the rocks to allow them to use the advantage of their much greater firepower and limitless ammunition.

"Busca. Whatever happens this day, you will always be my son."

"I am honored to be your son," I say. "You helped me find my father and have taught me more than I could ever have hoped to learn back in Yale. I will always treasure the stories you told me."

"And treasure your own story, Busca. However it turns out. I must go now."

"Go? Where?"

"Wherever my dreams lead. I am not destined to fight this day and my story does not end here, therefore I must go." Wellington turns and begins heading down the hill.

"Wait," I shout after him. "You can't go down there."

"Am I safer up here?" he asks over his shoulder, and then he's gone into the gloom. I try to follow, but the boy hangs on to my leg.

I lean on a rock and peer down. The land is gradually brightening, although it's still hard to make out any details. The soldiers are forming up in loose order, ready to move toward the hill. I try to count the figures, but it's difficult. There must be around a hundred in the area I can see, which means, if they completely surround our hill, which I'm certain they do, there must be three or four hundred soldiers in total. Against them we have possibly fifty surviving warriors with, at most, three or four rounds of ammunition each.

Eventually, I see a dark shape detach itself from the deeper shadows at the base of the hill. The figure makes no attempt at concealment and strides straight out onto the plain. I hold my breath as the figure approaches the soldiers, waiting for the gunshot. Nothing happens. Wellington moves through the loose line of soldiers and off across the plain toward the rising sun.

I shake my head in wonder, although there's little about Wellington that still surprises me. Conceivably the soldiers didn't see him. Perhaps they couldn't believe that a single old man would do such a thing and assumed he was a scout. Maybe it really just isn't Too-ah-yay-say's day to die.

＋═

It's full daylight by the time the soldiers get in among the rocks on the lower slopes of the hill.

As they approach, they are met by a volley of rifle fire, but it's not repeated and the firing from the rocks soon becomes ragged and then ceases altogether. A few wounded soldiers are being tended to out on the plain, but the advance never slows.

The soldiers are close together now, helping each other root out warriors from their hiding places. The firing is sporadic and all coming from the soldiers. Most of the women and children have moved closer to the top of the hill. The boy and I stay where we are. There seems little point in moving, whatever happens will happen wherever we are.

Whether I live or die will depend on the nature of the soldier who finds me and how quickly I can explain who I am in Spanish. At first glance, it's impossible to tell I am not an Apache beneath the dirt and ragged clothes. My hair is not dark and too short for most of the warriors, but I doubt if anyone will stop and ask me about that. The boy and I huddle and wait.

The soldier and Ghost Moon arrive at the same time. For an instant we all stare at each other. Time stops. I notice that the soldier is older than me and has a straggly dark mustache. His uniform is dirty and stained with blood. Ghost Moon holds my Colt in his left hand. I wonder why we can't just stay like this. Nothing need happen. No one needs to die. But the soldier raises his rifle.

The heavy bullet from the Colt tears into the soldier's chest, hurling him back behind the rock. My ears ring and the acrid smell of gunpowder irritates my nose.

"Go!" Ghost Moon is beside me, pointing up the hill. He jumps onto the rock and fires two rapid shots down the hill.

Before I can move, a bullet catches Ghost Moon in the side; its impact doubles him over. Almost immediately a volley of three more shots rings out. His body jerks convulsively, and he drops the revolver with a clatter onto the stone and falls on the far side of the rock.

I grab the boy and we scramble over the stony ground, keeping as low as possible. Women and children crouch behind almost every rock. There is no panic and they watch us pass in silence. One girl stares at me particularly intently as I pass. I smile weakly but receive no response.

At last we reach the open area we were in at dusk last night. Victorio is there, along with several warriors, most of whom are wounded. Victorio himself has a large bloodstain on his left thigh and leans heavily on his other leg. The warriors are singing in low modulated voices, eyes closed, softly stamping their feet in time.

The boy and I watch. After a moment, Victorio stops singing and opens his eyes. "Busca," he addresses me, "how close are the soldiers?"

"Close," I tell him.

"Too-ah-yay-say?"

"He escaped to the east," I reply.

Victorio nods. "He will meet with Nana and the others. Perhaps the old men will continue the fight."

"Ghost Moon is dead," I say.

"It is as he would wish." A gunshot sounds close by. "Do you still have the knife you defeated Ghost Moon with?" Victorio asks.

"Yes." I pull the knife from my belt.

Victorio holds out his hand and I pass the knife over. He turns it and looks at it thoughtfully. "It is a good knife," he says. He looks up at me. "You look sad, Busca. Do not mourn. Sing with happiness. My spirit and those of all on this hill go to a better place. Remember what you have seen and heard."

Only now do I notice that Victorio is holding the knife in two hands, the point against his chest.

Holding his body straight, he falls forward onto a low rock, forcing the long knife blade into his chest.

I don't have time to react before the soldiers are among us, shooting wildly at the wounded warriors. One man aims his rifle at me, but the boy throws himself between us shouting, "*Él es americano. Me salvó la vida. No lo mate!*"

The soldier stops, and I sink to the ground with relief, exhaustion and sadness. The story is finished.

# Chihuahua City, Mexico

21 October, 1880

Darkness is falling outside and a girl is busy lighting the lamps around us. The room is filling with shadows to hide the ghosts I have been remembering. I feel worn out.

"When the soldiers brought me down the hill, I felt as if I was back in one of my dreams. The rocks and ground were indeed splashed with blood. Soldiers were busy taking scalps from dead warriors, finishing off the wounded and collecting the surviving women and children.

"I saw one woman with a bullet wound in her shoulder trying to shield the girl who had stared at me on the way up the hill. Two soldiers hauled her off. One killed the wounded woman with his rifle butt while the other dragged the child down the hill to join the other captives."

"The girl in the corral who was watching us?" Santiago asks.

"Yes," I reply. "I wish I could do something to help her."

Santiago sits silently for a long time, watching the girl light the lamps. When she is done, he orders some spicy stew, tortillas and a bottle of mescal. When she is gone, he turns to me. "That is a very powerful story, James Doolen."

I nod, too drained by the telling to speak.

"You are privileged," he continues. "You have known some remarkable people."

"They're all dead," I say bitterly.

"We all die," Santiago says with a weak smile. "Some in battle, some peacefully in bed. Who is to say which is the luckier? But your friend Too-ah-yay-say was right—you are the keeper of the stories of those who died on the hill at Tres Castillos. Already lies are being told. I heard that a soldier is already claiming that he shot and killed Victorio."

"That's a lie!"

"I know that now," Santiago says, "but only because you told me the truth. That is why you must remember. You know the truth."

"It's hard. The memories are painful."

"The truth often is, but we must not forget the truth simply because it is painful to remember."

"I suppose," I say.

The girl returns with the stew, and we eat in silence. Santiago pours himself a generous glass of mescal; I decline the fiery liquid. When we are done, my friend wipes his lips, takes a long drink and sits back. He looks tired.

"There is another thing," Santiago says. "You said that Lozen escorted a woman and child back north to the reservation."

"Yes," I say, suddenly worried that Santiago was about to tell me of yet another tragedy.

"Victorio's sister left the band, even though she was their eyes and ears, because she believed that the infant was more important, that the child was the future of her people?"

"That's what she said when she left."

"What would you do if the girl in the corral was free and in your care?"

I think for a long time, a bit confused by Santiago's question. "Take her back to her people," I say eventually.

"Which of her people? Nana in the Sierra Madre or the reservation at Blazer's Mill?"

I give that question some thought as well. Nana and those who survived Tres Castillos, because they were away hunting, and Juh's band, are the only sizeable numbers of free Apaches left. But what is their future? It's a brutal life on the run. However skillful the leaders of the past have been—Managas Coloradas, Cochise, Victorio—all have been hunted down eventually. It's only a matter of time before Nana, Juh and Geronimo, if Lozen persuades him to join, will be as well. "I would take her to the reservation."

Santiago nods in agreement. "That is a good decision. Now, I have a full belly. If you would fill my glass, I will sit here in comfort while you do something for me."

"Of course," I say, moving round the table and pouring a measure of the amber liquid into Santiago's glass.

"Go to our room. In the bottom drawer of the table beside the bed, you will find a leather pouch. In it there are gold coins, all the money I have saved over the years. Some is owed to the hotel and for this excellent meal, but there will be enough left to purchase the girl at the slave auction tomorrow."

Santiago raises his hand to prevent my protestations. "I have no need of money anymore and no one to whom I can leave it. If I give it to you, perhaps some small good may come from this tragedy. Take her back to her people. Lozen was right, one child is the future, and perhaps the best we can hope for is to save one child at a time.

"On your journey, if you have enough words, tell her some of the story you have told me so that she also will remember."

I stand and look at Santiago. His suggestion makes sense and it thrills me. At last, something positive I can do. One child at least will not be sold into slavery.

"Are you certain?" I ask.

"I have never been more certain of anything," Santiago says with a smile. "Now go and fetch the money."

I turn toward the stairs, my step lighter than it has been in a long time. I barely hear Santiago say, "Goodbye," and I mumble something over my shoulder about being back in a moment. I climb the stairs two at a time, find the leather pouch and return.

At first I think Santiago has drifted off to sleep while I was gone, but then I see that his glass of mescal has slipped off the arm of his chair and lies broken on the floor.

I hurry over, but there's nothing to do. Santiago sits in the deep armchair, his hands on his lap and a faint smile on his lips. He has gone to be with Maria.

"I will do as you ask. You have given me back a purpose I have not had since I first came here searching for my father. I will buy the girl out of slavery and take her home. Thank you, old friend." I turn away. There are things to do, arrangements to be made.

Along with The Desert Legends Trilogy, **JOHN WILSON** has written more than thirty books for juveniles, teens and adults. His self-described "addiction to history" has resulted in many award-winning novels that bring the past alive for readers young and not-so-young. Wilson spends significant portions of the year traveling across the country speaking in schools, leaving his audiences excited about our past and its relevance to our lives today.

www.johnwilsonauthor.com

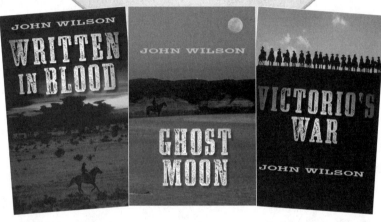

The following is an excerpt from *Death on the River,*
another exciting novel by **JOHN WILSON**.

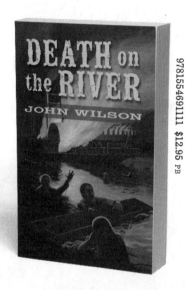

9781554691111 $12.95 PB

C aptured and confined to the Confederate prison
camp at Andersonville in June 1864, young Jake
Clay forms an unlikely alliance with Billy Sharp,
an unscrupulous opportunist who teaches him to survive
no matter what the cost. By war's end Jake is haunted by
the ghosts of those who've died so he could live. Now his
fateful journey home will come closer to killing him than
Andersonville did, but it will also provide him with one
last chance at redemption.

# JUNE 1865

# ONE 👉

I pull back the thin blanket and swing my legs over the edge of the bed. When I stand up, the tiled floor feels icy cold on my bare feet, but that's good—it reminds me that I'm alive.

There's a pile of clothes on the table by the bed. They're not mine; they were dropped off by a smiling nun who went round the ward asking if any of us needed anything. I said I wanted clothes and a pair of shoes, and her smile broadened so far that I thought her face would split. The guy in the bed beside me said he wanted his legs back, and she hurried off to help someone else.

I begin to dress, slowly because my hands are still sore. The legless guy turns his head. "Where you going?" he asks.

"Home," I say.

"Where's home?"

"Upstate New York," I answer as I painfully button my pants.

"That's a long way from Memphis."

I nod.

"You walking all that way?" he asks.

"Expect so."

"Lucky bastard," he says.

I pull on the shoes the nun brought. They're a surprisingly good fit.

"City shoes," the man says. "Won't last long on the road."

"I'll worry about that when I have to."

I shake his hand. It hurts, but then I'm used to pain.

"Think about me when you get blisters," he says with a bitter laugh.

"I will." I smile back.

I plan to walk north until I get home. It's not much of a plan. I've got some money, my discharge pay and a piece of paper that says that Jake Clay is no longer needed by the Union army. I'll scrounge or buy what food I can and sleep rough when I have to.

Walking all that way is a strange thing to do, but it's perfect for me. I want to go home, but I'm scared of getting there. Walking is slow enough that I can feel I'm going home but still postponing the arrival to the distant future.

At least I won't be alone.

The War between the States has been over for only two months, and the roads and rivers are clogged with men traveling in all directions. Most of them will make it home one way or another. That's the easy part. It's what you bring home inside your head that's the problem.

My hope is that the long walk will give me a chance to sort out what is going on in *my* head. Walking has always calmed me, helped me see things rationally. Maybe the miles and the dust will wear off the past I carry like a weight on my back. Make me forget the twelve months since I first went into battle that hopeless, bloody day at Cold Harbor. Make me forget the things I have seen, the things I have done, the ghosts who haunt my dreams. I can never go back to being the naïve kid I was before then, but with luck I can move forward.

I hope, but I don't know. Perhaps it's not possible to forget that you've been to Hell.